# ARIZONA AMES
# RIDES AGAIN

In his famous novel ARIZONA AMES, Zane Grey told of how young Rich Ames came to lead the life of a range drifter after a youthful gunfight left two men dead. Ames' skill with a sixgun came to dominate his life and spread his reputation throughout the West. Time after time in those lawless days, Arizona Ames rode into trouble — and when he rode out, the world was shy one or more badmen.

Now Arizona Ames rides again, in a new series of adventures created by Zane Grey's son, Romer Zane Grey.

# ZANE GREY'S ARIZONA AMES:

---

# GUN TROUBLE

# IN

# TONTO BASIN

## Romer Zane Grey

**Based on characters created by Zane Grey.**

**LEISURE BOOKS**  **NEW YORK CITY**

A LEISURE BOOK

Published by

Dorchester Publishing Co., Inc.
6 East 39th Street
New York, NY 10016

Printed in the United States of America

# Contents

# GUN TROUBLE
# IN
# TONTO BASIN

# I

As Arizona Ames rode away from Troublesome Valley through the night's darkness, he shut his eyes, and the desert through which he was riding seemed ablaze again with sunset colors—purple and saffron and gold—in an inward vision that made the darkness vanish.

When Ames opened his eyes again, the night seemed to have become even darker. Each sharp rise in the trail was more difficult to make out, each boulder and crag and sun-bleached steer's antler seemed to loom in the night with the ghostly indistinctness of a giant's skeleton spread out across the plain and crumbling, blending with the dust, at every joint.

Then, abruptly, the moon came out from behind a cloud and a long line of snow-fringed mountains came dimly into view far to the west. To the north and east purple canyons bisected miles upon miles of open desert, covered, here and there, with wide areas of silver grass and cactus growths much taller than a man.

The moon was still shining down brightly when he descended from his horse and built his first campfire since he had put the town, with all of its tragic memories behind him—or tried to—and ridden out upon the plain with his destination still not quite decided upon in his mind.

He was a stricken and tormented man, for the girl he had loved more than his own life had been killed by a bullet—not even aimed at her—before they could become man and wife.

He had no sooner gathered brushwood, lit the camp-fire and eased himself down to rest before it than all of the memories came rushing back.

He could see her face in the dancing, high-leaping flames. "Esther," he murmured, in a choked voice, aloud to the shadows. "Why did it have to happen? Oh, God, why? If we could have had just one week, a few hours even, in our own home."

Arizona Ames did not often talk that way, to himself or otherwise, for he was a rigidly self-disciplined man. But now, for the first time since he had held Esther Halstead for the last time in his arms, his shoulders slumped a little and his big-framed body was racked by sobs.

Ames did not remain by the fire until it had dwindled to glowing embers. Even if some wild creature of the night had been encircling the camp site with bared fangs he would, he knew, have resisted an impulse to lean forward and toss some more brushwood into the flames to make them leap high again.

Twenty minutes after he had descended from Cappy, his patient mount, he was dousing the fire and re-saddling the horse again, to resume his journey through the dark night.

Action was preferable to sitting before a campfire torturing himself with the memory of what might have been.

He froze in the act of drawing up a cinch, his hand

10

darting instantly to his gunbelt. Somewhere in the darkness that encompassed him a horse whinnied.

Then a voice that he recognized came out of the night and he swung abruptly about, his posture no longer strained.

"Ames! Arizona Ames! Where are you standing? I can't see you with that fire doused!"

It was the voice of Fred Halstead, Esther's brother. Ames had rescued Fred from a gang of cattle thieves who had been rustling his father's steers and who had come close to putting a quick end to his life.

So the lad had trailed him. Out of sympathy for his loss, Ames wondered, or because he didn't want the man who had almost become his brother-in-law to go riding off without at least a warm handclasp and expression of gratitude to remember him by.

"I'm right here, Fred!" Ames called, kicking the fire back to life again. "I was just getting set to ride on."

A young man, whose features would have been handsome if he had not been so weary-looking and haggard-eyed, came into view at the rim of the light cast by the rekindled fire, leading his horse.

There was a twisted smile on his face as he nodded at the older man. "Where are you headed for?" he asked bleakly. "You just rode off without letting anyone know. When I returned to the ranch house I found you gone."

"Where am I headed?" Ames muttered. "Hellbent to nowhere, maybe."

"I wish I could say I know how you feel," the youth replied. "But that would be a lie. Esther and I were very close, but I was just her brother. With you—" He let the words trail off.

"Some people claim I never let anything tear me apart," Ames said. "They don't know how mistaken they are."

A great many other contradictory ideas were held about the lean, broad-shouldered man who stood by the fire, a strand of blond hair falling down over his forehead.

There were lawless men who had reason to fear him who did not hesitate to brand Ames a gunslinger as reckless as themselves, a man without scruples and without remorse, and who looked forward to the day when his luck—or what they thought of as his luck—would run out.

But to a great many men and women, the oposite of lawless, he had earned not only the respect which was accorded him throughout the West, but the kind of affection and admiration which can set a man apart in a special way. Many people, in short, thought of Arizona Ames as a man of quiet strength, with a warm and generous heart.

There were a few, of course, who were convinced that he was more of a legend than a living man. For only a legend could vanish and reappear, dissolve in desert mists one moment and come riding the next with six-guns blazing, straight into the teeth of danger.

Although the youth who had emerged into the firelight leading his horse had known Ames long and well, he was looking at him now as if the legend idea could not be completely set aside.

Ames smiled briefly, showing strong teeth. "I had to leave, Fred," he said. "I just couldn't stay there any longer."

"I understand," Fred Halstead said awkwardly.

12

"But I was kind of disturbed when you left without saying goodbye. After all you did for me—"

"I told your father how it was. He said he'd take care of the farewells for me."

"He did. But like I said, when I came back and found you gone I was worried, because I was afraid you might not even stop to set a campfire. And I had to overtake you, arizona. I've got something for you."

"Before you tell me what it is, there's something I'm damned curious about. How did you ever manage to trail me?"

Young Halstead grinned. "You taught me all I know about trackin', Arizona. You should have known I'd put it to good use."

When Fred Halstead smiled he bore a striking resemblance to Esther, and Ames looked away quickly. He swallowed hard.

"I got a letter for you," Halstead went on. "That's why I trailed you, Arizona." He reached inside his shirt and brought out a white envelope which he passed on to Ames.

It was from the Tonto Basin. With a stir of expectation, Arizona Ames recognized his twin sister's handwriting. Nesta Ames Playford was a faithful correspondent but in the last fourteen years Ames had not lingered long in one place. His last letter from Nesta had been dated two years previously.

Ames tore open the flap, took out the letter and began reading, the firelight casting a glow on the paper.

*Dear Rich: I hope this letter doesn't reach you too late. Wherever you are, brother, and whatever you're doing, you must have felt my prayers. We need you now, here in Tonto Basin. Things are going on that are beyond me. My husband—I know you remember Sam Playford—is a changed man. He's so unlike the way he was when you knew him it's frightening. I know it is dangerous for you to come back, Rich, but we desperately need you. Please hurry. Love, Nesta.*

Ames looked up from the letter to see Fred Halstead watching him anxiously.

"Bad news, Arizona?" the youth asked.

Ames nodded and stood up, abruptly thrusting the letter into his pocket. He knew that Nesta would never have written to him in such a vein if it had not been important.

"From home," he said briefly, and the word had a lonely sound to him. "I'd just about decided to go back anyway. This simply means I'll have to hurry it some."

"Anything I can do?" Halstead asked.

Ames shook his head. "You might as well camp here with me tonight. You can ride back in the morning." He had a soft, slow way of talking that masked his sudden anxiety concerning Nesta and her family.

"You're all saddled up," Fred said.

"I told you I was fixing to ride on," Ames said bleakly. "But I guess a few hours more here won't really make a big difference." He unsaddled the big black horse and prepared his bed while Fred Halstead did the same.

In their blankets, with the campfire flickering out, Halstead said, "All of us, Father and the kids, appreciate all you did for us. We can't get over what happened." He stopped speaking when his voice broke.

Ames wondered if he could get over it, too. Every-

14

thing had been so wonderful. After years of wandering he'd become convinced that he'd found the right woman and the right place.

The agony of remembering was almost more than he could bear. After the trouble with the rustlers, after he'd saved Fred's life, the elder Halstead had made him a full partner in the ranch in Troublesome. He and Esther had planned to get married and visit his sister and her family in Arizona. They were in Yampa, the mining camp that was a half day's ride from the ranch when one of the rustlers, filled with vengeance, had ambushed Ames. Esther had gotten in the way of a bullet meant for him. She had died in his arms there on Yampa's dusty street, and part of Arizona Ames had died with her.

"It was what I wanted to do," Ames said, his voice stern with emotion. "Go to sleep, Fred."

"Why can't I go with you to Arizona?"

"You can't leave the ranch. Your father needs you. And there's that little girl, Fred, Bindy Wood—the one you're going to marry. You can't leave all that."

"I can always come back."

"Go to sleep," Ames repeated.

Halstead finally dozed off. And when he awoke in the morning Arizona Ames was gone.

As he saddled his horse, Fred Halstead remembered the day that Ames had appeared on the ranch. The man had an amazing effect on the problems that beset the Halsteads. The ranch was failing, and Fred's father had been in the clutches of the notorious Hensler gang, whose viciousness spanned more than one generation. Arizona Ames had pulled them all out of a nasty hole.

"He's one man I'll never forget," the youth prom-

ised himself as he turned his horse toward Troublesome.

## II

Arizona Ames came out of the foothills of southeastern
Utah that were ablaze with color and began his crossing
of the desert. He was going on a straight line for the
Tonto Basin, and the further he traveled the more
eagerly he hungered for the sight of the basin.

He had sighted smoke signals from the flat-topped
buttes to the east twice after entering the desert. There
were Apache, but usually they roamed far to the south
of this place.

In the eyes of a passing stranger he would have been
instantly recognized for what he was, a man born to
the saddle. As Cappy plodded through the sand, Ames
experienced no discomfort from the deep, unbroken
heat. With an easy manner he headed his horse toward
the corbelled roof of a wood-and-mud hut in the distance. Sheep were strung out all around the hut.

There would be water there, he thought.

The shepherd arose from the shadow of a bush and
came toward him as he neared the hut. "Good day,
*Senor*," he said in Spanish.

Ames returned the greeting in the same tongue and
dismounted, unsaddled his horse and rubbed Cappy's
back where heat and pressure had caused the animal
discomfort.

"I would be honored, *Senor*, if you would share
my supper."

"Thank you," Ames said, smiling. "I'm sure tired
of my own cooking." He squatted beside the fire the

16

Mexican had prepared, and nodded toward the distant buttes. "You see the smoke?" he asked.

The shepherd raised dark, frightened eyes to Ames and nodded. "*Si*. They take a white man, *Senor*. They call in other members of the tribe to witness the pleasure they will have."

Arizona Ames nodded. It wouldn't be pleasant for the man they'd captured. He found himself wondering how much time it would slow him to go up there. He shook his head, his face grim. Nesta needed him more than any stranger.

And yet, as he ate tortillas and mutton and drank goat's milk, he was unable to rid his mind of the mental picture of a mortally terrified man tied to the stakes, awaiting torture as only the Apache knew how to administer it.

Night came down fast in the desert.

Afterward, while the Mexican softly strummed a guitar and the sheep made soft sounds in the night, Ames tried again to put from his mind all thought of riding toward the buttes. He didn't succeed.

The Mexican laid down his guitar. "You are not leaving tonight, *Senor*?" he asked incredulously.

Ames waved toward the butte. "I've got to see if I can do something about the white man," he said.

An hour later, he was approaching the buttes, after having thanked the Mexican for his hospitality. He paid him the equivalent of the night's lodging he might otherwise have requested, since he was in need of rest for the long ride ahead and knew that sleeping under a roof could do more for a man than a restless night under the stars.

Presently he dismounted from his horse and led the animal. He stopped once and stifled a whinny. Cappy

17

could smell water and Ames knew he was nearing the Apache camp. He tied Cappy to a bush and went on, more slowly now.

He found the camp near morning. The Apache were sleeping, and they obviously felt secure, for no guards had been posted.

Ames squatted in the shadow of a pinon and looked the camp over. He counted ten warriers and twenty women and children. A few sheep the band had stolen were tethered near the center of the camp. The Apache had several burros and a few horses.

The white prisoner was staked out on the ground, stripped naked from crown to toe, not sleeping, for in the dim light Ames caught the flash of his eye whites. There had been a fire near the man's head but the Apache had apparently allowed it to die out. They would resume their torture later.

Ames removed his boots, so that he could move more quietly. He circled the camp, screened by the pinons until he was as near the prisoner as he could get without leaving cover. He knelt there, listening. The animals made scraping sounds nearby. The wind was dead. There was a smell of earth and pine garlanded with the unwashed bodies scattered in the grove of pinon.

Ames rose, crouching and went swiftly to the side of the staked-out man. He leaned over him with a hand ready to muzzle any outcry.

The man's eyes rolled up at him, and closed quickly again in understanding.

A slash of the knife freed the bearded man. He came erect, rubbing his hands and then his ankles where the rawhide throngs had cut into his flesh.

Ames pulled him toward the shelter of the pinons,

half-supporting him. He appeared stiff from having been staked out for so long a time. He had not uttered a sound, other than the sharp intake of his breath when he had first looked at Ames.

An Apache rose from sleep in one motion. The cry died in his throat as Ames fired. The sleeping sounds erupted in a tumult of shouting as Ames and the bearded man went through the pinons.

A stocky, broad-shouldered Apache came careening through the brush and Ames fired again. The Indian doubled up squealing.

"Let's get out of here!" Ames urged, his voice hoarse with strain. "That I'm most happy to do," the other muttered.

As they broke free of the pinon a bullet whistled through the pine needles, and a gun roared behind them. Ames paused for an instant but saw nothing to shoot at.

They went on, from one clump of brush to another, keeping themselves screened as much as possible.

A scatter of shots came from behind them. A dark shape arose off to one side and again the sixgun in Ames' hand barked sharply. The leaping form folded into the ground.

"Waaah!" Three Apache with three cartridges! That sure is some shootin'."

Several shrieking forms came out of the night, and Ames emptied his gun. Three braves went down, and others swarmed forward. One caught Ames around the waist and they wrestled into the brush. A steel knife flashed, but it was stopped in midair as Ames grabbed the man's wrist. Ames drew back his leg, and drove his knee into the Apache's crotch. The Indian gave a high-pitched scream, and dropped.

Someone was yelling. It wasn't the Indians. The man Ames had rescued shouted an eerie battle cry and the Apache faded back. Ames ran, his legs pumping toward the man standing naked in the brightening light.

. Cappy was half-rearing and Ames untied the horse, and swung up to disengage a stirrup for the man he'd rescued. Swiftly they turned the horse away from the buttes and red canyons, and out into the desert.

Ames stopped only long enough to take some spare clothes from his saddle pack and gave them to the man, who said, "Name's Herman Hammicker. Here's one old hoss is mighty proud to know you!"

He was tall, big of bone, with a hawk nose and full black beard. His small, deep-set gray eyes twinkled humorously. He reminded Ames of his old boyhood friend, Cappy Tanner, dead these many years.

They rode on, and as the sun rose higher the wind came up, lifting sheets of sand, whining and moaning over the sage. Ames did not see enough grass to nourish a goat. He protected himself as well as he could by covering his nose with his handkerchief, and pulling his hat down low over his face. Hammicker had wrapped a big bandana around his head.

"We gonna have to find shelter," Hammicker said, in a muffled voice.

"Keep looking," Ames said.

Toward the middle of afternoon the horse left the sand for rocks. Ames crossed a faint trail and turned into it, climbing as they entered a canyon. The low walls shut off the wind and dust. Ames pushed back his hat and pulled the neckerchief down around his neck. He wiped his face with his sleeve.

The narrow canyon they had entered grew deeper and wider. Ames discovered that there were fresh

20

tracks in the trail. He slipped a leg over the horn and slid to the ground. Hammicker got down slowly and painfully. He had not complained, but Ames knew the Apache had hurt him during the hours of torture.

"This canyon leads up through the rim and into Tonto," Ames said.

"That's where I'm heading."

They made camp and Ames got meat and bread out of his saddle bags and shared it with Hammicker. They washed it down with water from the canteen.

Hammicker leaned back with a sigh. "Seems like I ain't thanked you yet. What're you called, friend?"

Ames had purposely allowed his beard to grow out. It was luxuriant and yellow as wheatstraw. He debated whether it would be wise to tell Hammicker the truth. He wanted to return to the Tonto Basin without revealing his identity until he'd had a chance to size things up. He glanced at Hammicker.

"You don't have to tell me nothin', son," the latter said, as if aware of his thoughts. Aside from the fact that this lean, tough man had saved his life, Hammicker appeared to be attracted by the fact that there was a wrenching air of sadness and tragedy in Ames' expression.

"I was wondering how the Apache got you," Ames drawled.

"Yeah, that's a story now. I'm a trapper—" He stared at Ames perplexedly. "You was gonna say somethin'?"

Ames shook his head. "You remind me of an old friend, Cappy Tanner. He was a trapper, too. I knew him when I was a kid. Named my horse after him, in fact."

21

"Yeah. Wal, how'd you know them red buggers had me?"

"A Mexican sheepherder told me."

"That must be old Juan Tomas. Yeah, I'd just had some good tortillas and mutton with him. They took me not a mile from where I left Juan. I lost everythin' I had, and they were fixin' to give me an Apache beauty treatment—the rest of it, I mean."

"You ever been in the Tonto Basin?"

"I sure have. Bought my supplies in Shelby a few times."

"Ever hear of the Ames family over that way?"

"Who hasn't? Some of them are still there, as I recollect."

"Who?" Ames' penetrating blue eyes bored into those of the old man.

"Man, I ain't tryin' to twist yore tail. I mean I hear things even an old coot like me what don't visit the settlements much. There's this widder woman up there—Arizona Ames' maw. An' his two little twin sisters, Mescal and Manzanita. His grown-up sister married a feller named Playford. He's the biggest man in the Basin."

"In size, that is?"

"Size, money, cows, land. You put a tag on it, an' he's the big one, son."

"Reckon we better mosey on," Ames said laconically, rising.

When Ames turned, Hammicker saw the silver letter A embedded in the black leather.

Ames saw Hammicker's gaze resting on the black holster. He unbuckled the gunbelt and took his knife and prised out the silver A. Remembering as he did it that old Cappy Tanner had brought him the revolver

22

and gunbelt and a .44 Winchester on that day long ago when the old trapper had returned to the Basin—for the last time, as it turned out.

The news that his mother was alive and well had come as an overwhelming relief to Ames. He'd feared that perhaps the unhappiness she'd suffered had hastened her death. She'd been widowed in the Pleasant Valley war when Arizona was very small, and then her only son had been forced to flee the Basin after a shooting scrape.

It was twilight when they reached the summit. The air was cool and the wind whipped at the pine thickets. It was too dark to see any of the country below and Ames could scarcely restrain his longing for a sight of it. He wanted bright daylight to get his first glimpse of the land he loved.

"We'd best make camp right here," he said. "We're going to have to outfit you in Shelby, because a man without a pair of boots is plain handicapped."

"I guess you could say that, son. But there's another way of looking at it. I'm glad I still got my feet."

Ames chuckled and then stopped short, surprised at the sound. He'd not seen or heard anything to cause him to laugh since Esther's tragic death.

Hammicker put a kindly hand on Ames' shoulder. "Son, whatever it is that's diggin' you, worryin' about me ain't goin' to help." His hand tightened on Ames' shoulder. "As for boots, why I ain't got a thin dime to pay for 'em."

"I'm planning to stake you," Ames said shortly.

He set about taking care of his horse and making camp. He was touched by the old man's gratitude, and found himself remembering Cappy Tanner. Hammicker reminded him of his old friend.

He sensed that he was going to need a friend. Perhaps in Herman Hammicker he'd found one.

## III

Ames awoke to the old, familiar sigh of the wind in the pines. It was music he'd missed over the years. The sweet, dry, pungent odors of the evergreens were medicine, soothing and relieving his wounded spirit.

Hammicker, rolled up in a ball on the other side of the campfire, stretched mightily and groaned. "Man, this sure is fine country!" he exclaimed.

After breakfast they walked down into the Basin. The horse was too trail-weary to carry double, and Ames wanted his passage to be slow, as he savored every moment of it. Deer, bear and wild turkeys went away before them.

The trail led out of the deep shade of the forest into open sunight that shone on rough oak ridges, with dense thickets in the gulches between. Here and there glimpse of the rough canyon country framed themselves in notches of the ridges—wild dark canyons, suggestive of the haunts of bear and mountain lion.

At last the whole length of Mescal Ridge stretched away before Ames' eager gaze. Silver and black and green, a mighty hog-back among all those Tonto ridges, it stretched out below them, open to their gaze. Cattle and deer dotted the gray patches of grass. This was where the Ames family had lived since his father had migrated from Texas when Arizona had been a small boy.

From where he stood he could see the colorful flat nestling under the beetling brow of Mescal Ridge. The log cabin where he had lived shone brown and tiny beside the three great spruce trees. The garden was still there, a green square on the land. The railfences which he had built with the help of Cappy Tanner, his old trapper friend, were vine-covered.

Hammicker sighed and looked at Ames. "Son, I'd say you been here afore this."

Ames was silent, remembering how it had been that last month in this land with Nesta's entrapment by the blackest of scoundels, Lee Tate, and its tragic consequences. He'd killed Tate in a gunfight that had freed Nesta to marry big Sam Playford. In the same gunfight he'd wounded another Tate and killed the sheriff, Jeff Stringer.

He wondered if the Tates were still looking for him to return. They were a grudge-holding family, with feuding in their tainted blood.

"We better get on down," Ames said heavily.

"You goin' to go by your old home?"

Ames gave him a startled look. "Just what do you mean by that, old timer?"

Hammicker chuckled deep in his throat. "Shoot. The old horse ain't real bright but I can put two and two together."

"Which two and two is that, precisely?"

"Wal, that silver A on your holster, for one thing. And one time when I was in Shelby a feller pointed out a woman named Nesta Playford. He said she was Arizona Ames' twin sister. She sure looked almighty like you, son."

"And I wanted to come back without anybody knowing," Ames said sadly.

"Wal, as far as I'm consairned you have, Ames. Nobody's ever goin' to pry the truth out of me."

"Can I bank on that, Herman?"

25

"You sure can, pard."

They shook hands.

The Ames cabin on the flats was a powerful attraction for Arizona but he forced himself to put aside his yearning to go there. There would be time for that later, he told himself, as he and Hammicker made their way slowly toward the town.

Shelby had changed little since Ames had left it on the run, more than a dozen years before. There was the same false-fronted buildings, new stores, tavern and saloon. The sound of hammer on an anvil made him wonder if Henry the blacksmith was still around. Henry had been a special friend of Cappy's.

Turner's—where Nesta and Sam had been brought together at a local wedding—had not changed. A liver-spotted brown hound lay sleeping in the sun in front of the sheriff's office. A tall, but corpulent man came to the door and looked at them curiously as Ames tied his horse to the rail in front of the merchandise store. A silver star gleamed on the fat man's black vest. He hesitated, and then came quickly down the steps and approached them. His attitude was unfriendly and authoritative.

"Strangers in town?" he asked, his eyes on Hammicker's bare feet.

"Complete," Ames said coolly.

Something in Ames' cool blue eyes—and in his voice—caused the sheriff to start perceptibly. He placed a pudgy hand on the butt of his gun as though to reassure himself. "Travelin' through or plannin' to light?" the sheriff asked bluntly.

"We haven't decided, sheriff," Ames said good-naturedly. "You check on everybody like this or on us because my friend's barefooted?"

The sheriff grunted. "How does it happen he's bare-footed?"

Hamicker cleared his throat. "Wal, it's like this, Sheriff, I met this feller and we got to arguin' about which one of us had the biggest feet."

"Don't give me no cock-an-bull story," the sheriff said, bluntly.

"Wal, yes sir. It was the Apaches, Sheriff. Bunch of them red devils had me staked out. My friend here come along just in time to save me."

"Then you ain't been together long?" the sheriff asked, his shrewd little black eyes darting from one to the other.

A few men walking down the street had paused to listen. They were silent, looking at each man as he spoke in turn. The sheriff was perspiring freely. He clearly had the feeling that these two wayfarers should be showing a little more respect for the Law than they had displayed. He cleared his throat.

'I'll be keepin' an eye on you," he said. 'Whilst you're in town, that is."

"Well, thank you, Sheriff," Ames said, and turned away.

"It's time we got ourselves outfitted and into tubs of hot water in the back room of the barbershop," he said to his new friend, the instant they were alone again.

'Wal, I reckon I can take it if you can," Herman grunted. "Truth is, I only take two baths a year whether I need 'em or not. And I've had my two this year."

The barber was still in business. Tom Melvin had aged considerably, and Ames watched him closely to see if there was a sign of recognition. Melvin had cut his hair many times in the past. But now the aging man, withered, white and slightly doddering, paid scant attention to him.

Afterward, clean and in new clothing, Hammicker and Ames went out on the street again. Ames said, "Well, friend, here's a stake for you." He gave the old trapper a twenty-dollar gold piece. "I'm leaving town, and I don't know when I'll see you again."

"Wish I could go with you," Hammicker said wistfully.

"There's just the one horse. And Cappy is getting kind of old to carry double."

"Wal, shoot, I wouldn't expect him to, son." Hammicker had spent too much time alone to relish the prospect of buddying up with anyone but Ames had seemingly put a spell on him. "You figurin' on lightin' some place, just send me word. If you need help I'll come runnin'."

Ames chuckled. "I don't know what I'm going to do first off," he said.

"I've seen a lot of tracks comin' in," Hammicker said reflectively. "I just might get a few traps and run a set-about."

"This used to be good trapping country," Ames said, nodding. "I noticed the tracks, too. You might do yourself some good. But twenty dollars is not much of a stake."

"I've always been a thrifty person," Hammicker said. "Reckon I can make do." He squinted at Ames. "I can't rightly thank you for all you done for me, pard. I'm no good when it comes to putting how I feel into words."

Ames walked quickly away, toward his horse. He was untying the animal when two girls mounted on

28

spirited pintos trotted down the street, and wheeled their mounts in before Frye's mercantile.

Ames watched them with a slowly quickening beat of his heart. The girls were Manzanita and Mescal, his younger sisters. They had been six years old when he'd fled the Basin. That was how many years ago? God, they had to be almost twenty. He swallowed hard as he watched them dismount, and tie their horses to the hitching rack in front of the store. They were beautiful, well-formed young women with the distinctive Ames light hair, and deep blue eyes.

They noticed him staring at them and he raised his hat.

"I wonder if you young ladies could direct me to Cappy Turner's place?" he asked, finding it difficult to control his voice.

"Uncle Cap?" It was Mescal who spoke—or was it Manzanita? "Why, he's been dead—" she looked at her sister.

"Six years," Manzi said quietly.

They stood regarding him curiously. Then Mescal spoke, "What did you want Mr. Tanner about?"

"Mescal!" Manzanita's voice was sharp. "It's not polite—"

"Yes, of course," she agreed, quickly. "I'm sorry."

"I just wanted to see the place. I'm thinking about buying it from Mr. Tanner's heirs."

The twins exchanged glances. "It's below Mescal Ridge, the other side of where we lie," Mescal said.

"And where do you live?" Ames asked, not wanting them to know how unnecessary the question was.

Mescal told him. "After you pass our clearing you follow the path above the creek. You come to a deep

29

pass and it let's you into Uncle Cappy's valley. His cabin is real nice. Our brother Rich used to go there often when—when he was here.''

"You'll have to excuse us, please," Manzanita said primly.

Ames mounted his horse and rode away with the two girls watching from the doorway of the mercantile store.

"Oh, what a handsome man!" Mescal exlaimed.

"Humph! Kind of old, if you ask me.''

"Well, yes, he must be thirty or more. But he's so nice looking—and with nice manners." She sighed.

"Yeah, he had a handsome face though.''

"Mescal, you simply think every man is—''

"I don't either!''

"Well, let's get our shopping done. Mother told us to hurry back.''

"Oh, there, twins," the sheriff called, and the two girls turned. "What'd that feller want with you?''

The girls glanced at each other and then back to Sheriff Cliff Fraser. "Oh, you mean that handsome stranger?" Mescal asked innocently.

"Yeah. That's him. What did he ask you? What did you talk about?''

"He wanted to know how to get to Cappy Tanner's old place.''

"Thats strange." Sheriff Fraser took off his hat, and scratched his head. He looked at them with his small black eyes. "You sure?''

"Of course we're sure," Manzanita said sharply. "Come along Mescal.''

The two girls went into the store, and White continued to look down the street where Ames had gone. Then sighing, he walked with his shambling gait kattycorner across the street and climbed the outside stairway to a small office over Melvin's barbershop and Molly's Millinery. It was one of the town's few two-story buildings and the top floor contained only that one small office which was occupied by a man named Slade Gorton, who was of considerable importance in the town.

The sheriff tapped on the door and called, "Mr. Gorton?"

A voice bade him come in. It was a deep, commanding voice.

The sheriff went in and stopped inside the door. The slim, darkly handsome owner of the voice stood at the window looking down into the street. Fraser was quite sure that Gorton had witnessed his encounter with the two strangers, and with the Ames twins.

"Well, Sheriff Fraser." Gorton's tone was ironic and bored.

Sheriff Cliff Fraser hastily closed the door. He noticed the huge shape of Sam Playford in a corner, slumped in a chair. "Uh, I didn't know you had a visitor," he said apologetically.

Gorton laughed, a thin slicing laugh with a jeering, demeaning note. "Don't mind him," he said.

He turned and surveyed the sheriff, an expensively-dressed man with a darkly handsome face that was damaged by its hardness and sly, shifty black eyes. "What do you want?"

Fraser blinked his eyes. "Couple of strangers in town," he said.

"That makes three this week. What're they doing here?"

"I dunno. The old one is wanderin' around and the

young one just rode out—after asking directions to Cappy Turner's place.''

Gortn jerked his head sharply. "Cappy Turner's place?" he asked in a soft voice. "Are you sure?"

When Fraser did not answer, Gorton went on in an angry voice. ''If you were half the sheriff you should be you'd run every one of these strangers out of town as soon as they show up.''

The sheriff knew that Gorton was agitated because a stranger was asking about Tanner's place. The old man had found gold on his place before he died and Gorton meant to get it in one way or another. That damned young couple, the Sullivans, had settled there and Gorton was having difficulty running them off. All these thoughts passed through the sheriff's mind before he spoke, again.

"That big one didn't appear to be the kind to run easy," he said sulkily.

"Looks like I'm paying the wrong man. Maybe I can get him for sheriff."

Fraser was silent.

"If you see him again tell him I want to have a talk with him," Gorton said.

"Yes, sir," Fraser replied.

Goton turned back to the window and placed his hands behind his back. He stood looking don into the street as Fraser turned and ambled out, closing the door softly behind him.

"You own the sheriff," Playford said heavily. "You don't need me, Gorton." There was a desperate edge to his voice.

Gorton didn't look at him. "You can go now, Sam. You're absolutely right. I *don't* need you. Not right now, I don't.''

Playford rose and walked like a man in his sleep to the door. He opened it, and his tread on the stairs was heavy-footed.

Two roughly dressed men came from an inner door and lounged into the room. They were unshaven and dirty, and Gorton's nose wrinkled at both the sight and smell of them. He looked at first one and then the other.

"You saw them. What about it?"

"The old man, Herman Hammicker, was the one we were trailin' when the Apaches got him. If he had any gold before, he sure ain't got it now."

"If he leaves town, follow him," Gorton said. "And now get the hell out of here. You both stink."

The two roughly dressed men hastily left the room.

Gorton opened a window until the wind washed the odor out. Then he closed the window, sat down at his desk, and leaned back with a sigh of satisfaction.

He'd not done so bad for a man on the run, he told himself. After killing the reckless fool of an engineer in a train robbery of the St. Louis and San Francisco express in Missouri he'd had a run of bad luck. That he had to admit. The police had hounded him relentlessly and finally cornered him in a boarding house in St. Louis. But it took the sting out of that to recall how he'd broken jail while awaiting trial and fled to Tucson, and made a stake there.

Eventually he had found himself in the Tonto Basin with a determination that this was where he was going to make it big. He meant to go for broke. He'd tackled the biggest man in the country, Sam Playford, hadn't he, and Playford was now eaing out of his hand.

With Playford in his pocket he was well on his way. Gorton's brow furrowed. Three strangers in town

33

in one week. Usually they got one or two a year, the nameless breed that were the scourge of he West.

He rose briskly, straightened his cravat and went down the stairs to the saloon to have his afternoon drink. He walked with a straight back, proud, even arrogant, and the people in Shelby looked at him respectfully and spoke of him with even more respect.

## IV

As Ames neared the flat where the home place was located his eagerness comunicated itself to Cappy. The horse pricked up its ears and whinnied.

He saw the log cabin shining brown through the trees. He touched Cappy with spurs, and the horse broke into a lope. He missed the welcome the dogs had accorded him long ago. The place was quiet in the afternoon sun. The sound of Cappy's hoofs brought Mrs. Ames to the doorway. She stood there, wiping flour from her strong brown arms. She was fifty-four, Ames remembered, and she was still handsome, her fair hair sprinkled with gray, tall and strong, a pioneer woman of the old pattern.

She watched him dismount and tie his horse with puzzled wonder in her deep blue eyes. Then she cried, "Rich!" and came running toward him, her arms outstretched.

He held her close in his arms, stroking her hair and murmuring he knew not what.

She stood back from him. "I dreamt about you last night. My nose's been itchin' this live-long day and I knowed somebody was comin'! But I didn't dream it would be you." She wiped tears from her eyes with

34

her apron. "You come right in the house this minute! You look so thin, I know you must be half-starved."

He laughed, holding her back, for she would have rushed straight into the cabin. "How'd you know it was me?"

She looked at him reproachfully. "My own son?"

"I saw the twins in town. They didn't turn an eyelash."

"You're forgetting how small they were when you went away. Anyway, when I saw you ridin' up I got a start. Nobody ever quite sat on a horse the way you do, Rich. You *are* hungry, aren't you, son?"

Ames knew his mother would never rest until she'd stuffed him with food. "As a bear," he replied.

"Then you come right in the house and put your feet under the table while I whip up somethin'."

Ames stood in the doorway, looking feelingly at the cabin. The living room extended the width of the dwelling and perhaps half its length. With a fire burning in the stone fireplace it was as he remembered it, cheery and comfortable. It also served as a dining room, but the two beds, one in each corner, had been removed, indicating the diminishing size of the family. A door near the chimney opened into the kitchen.

"Still the same old place," Mrs. Ames said cheerfully. "I don't cook on the fireplace any more." She pointed to a brightly polished stove with a warming oven and water reservoir. She walked to a sink and pumped a handle. "Sam put runnin' water in for me a few years back."

"How is Sam?" Ames tried to make his voice casual.

"Nesta told me she was writin' you to come, but I never believed you would."

Ames realized that his mother had purposely avoided answering his question and it disturbed him. But he let it pass.

"I wasn't exactly welcome back here," he said wryly.

"A lot of water has passed under the bridge," she said vaguely. Then she brightened. "Would you like a venison steak, Rich? Nesta's boy brought me a half a deer—oh, he's the hunter of the family now, Rich, just like you were at his age." Without waiting for an answer, she sliced a steak from a haunch.

"Good heavens, he's old enough to hunt?"

She nodded. "Hes thirteen an' a crack shot with a rifle."

"How about pistols?"

"Sam won't let him have one. He's wild to shoot a hand gun. Guess he's heard stories about—about Arizona Ames." She avoided meeting his gaze as she spoke the words, but he knew there was a look of dread in her eyes.

"Arizona Ames," he said softly. "How I hated that name. But it hung on, and couldn't shuck it off."

She placed steak and potatoes before him and began buttering biscuits, "If you want to help Sam and Nesta you'll need more than a fast draw, Rich." She caught herself up. "I shouldn't have said that. But it has always hurt me, the way things turned out. I should have known, though. Your grandfather, Caleb, was a fire-eater. Your Uncle Jess Ames was the fightin' Texan. I always knew you'd give gray hair, and you ain't disappointed me none."

"How about the Tates?" Ames asked, bringing up the subject of old enemies, dating back to the Pleasant Valley war, when cattlemen, sheepmen and rustlers

36

had almost killed each other off. Arizona Ames had lost his own father in that holocaust when he was very young. "There's Slink," his mother said with a grimace. "He's the last one and he's all crippled up from that—that gunfight."

The gunfight she mentioned was the one that had caused Arizona Ames to flee the Basin, and just the mention of it brought back bitter memories.

"The last Tate," he said musingly.

"Well, not exactly the last," his mother replied thoughtfuly. "There's Anna Belle, his daughter. But she ain't nothin' like the other Tates."

Arizona Ames kept silent. His mother, after her initial reticence, was beginning to talk and he let her talk as she willed, fearful that she'd stop and say no more.

"Sam Playford is a big man hereabouts now, Rich. But him and Nesta ain't happy. There's something worrying Sam, and he won't talk. He's always been so good to Nesta and the boy."

"He changed any in that respect?" mes asked.

Martha Ames shook her head. "No, but he's turned secretive and goes away for days at a time now. I thought maybe Slade Gorton was back of it. I don't know for certain."

"Slade Gorton? I think maybe I met him in Shelby. A slick, handsome dude with ruffles on his shirt."

She nodded. "Don't let them ruffles fool you, son. He's as dangerous a man as ever came to Arizona. He moved in right after you left and next to Sam, Gorton is the most powerful man in the Basin." She looked at him with dread and sorrow in her eyes. "Sometimes I think he's more powerful. Sam's afraid of him for reasons I don't know."

Ames pushed back his plate. "I don't want it known that I'm back," he said. "Not yet, anyway. I'd like to look around before it gets out that I'm here."

"It's hard to keep a secret in the Basin," she said.

He nodded. "Things haven't changed much in that respect, have they?"

"I reckon not," she said gloomily. She looked at him. "Where you goin' to stay, son?"

He shrugged his wide shoulders. "Camp out somewhere. There's room for a thousand men to hide out twenty or thirty miles from town."

"And you know all of them," she said with satifaction. "You better hustle now. The girls will be back any moment."

His mother had never wept, as far as he could remember. She didn't cry now. But she stood there looking at him with her bright bue eyes swimming with tears. He had an unutterable ache in his heart as he went out the door and mounted Cappy and turned toward the gloomy canyons that would shield him for the time being.

V

With the Mogallan Mesa at his back, Arizona Ames looked down on the mighty panorama of Tonto Basin. This was his home, his land, and he loved it mightily. He'd missed it every moment of the dangerous years he'd been away.

He scanned the innumerable ridges of the Basin which slanted downward like the ribs of a colossal whale. Down in the sheltered nooks the sycamore trees shone with green-gold leaves and the oaks smoldering in rich bronze, standing out vividly from the steel-gray shaggy slopes. He stiffened when he caught sight of a flash of movement along Tonto Creek.

He got his glasses from his pack and went back to his observation post and stretched out at full length. He put the glasses near the boiling white of rushing rapids. A horse appeared with the rider slumping in the saddle. Then another came into view and he sighed with disappointment.

The second rider was the old trapper, Herman Hammicker.

The two riders stopped and Ames adjusted the glasses again, bringing the distant figures into clearer focus. Hammicker waved his hand upward, his gaze on the Mescal Ridge where Ames was camped.

Another motion caught his eye. He swept the glasses past the two riders and far beyond where flurry of movement drew his attention. Two more riders were back there, keeping well behind Hammicker and his companion. Ames instantly sensed that they were advancing warily, in a skulking manner. Hammicker and his friend were being trailed.

As he watched, the two riders pulled into a draw and dismounted. From where they stood, Ames realized, they could watch the trail without being seen. He was satisfied that the two trailing riders had not spotted him.

Ames went down the faint trail to meet the two riders. Despite his tenseness and mounting uneasiness, he was still assimilating the sights, sounds and smells of the valley, and found them invigorating. The solitude of the slopes and valleys, the signs of wild game in the dust of the trail, the quarreling of the creek, the penetrating fragrance of pine and spruce, the brush, the dead leaves, the fallen cones, the mat of needles, were all proof that he had come home to the environment he loved best. His passage was silent because he had discarded his boots for soft leather moccasins.

He came out between gray-lichened rocks, listening to the crack of hoofs on rock down the trail beside the creek. Soon two riders emerged from the green; the first was a stranger. He stopped his horse and raised his hand. He was a tall, black-hatted man with a stern, brown face, clean-shaven except for a black handlebar mustache. The second rider was Hammicker.

"Wal, son, here I am, and damn glad to see you again," he said, swinging down and stepping forward to offer his hand.

Ames' cool glance went to the stranger as he shook hands with the old trapper. "You gave me away, Herman," he said.

"Wait son, before you go jumpin' to conclusions," the tall man said and dismounted.

"This is Cap'n Will Kirk," Hammicker said. "When he convinced me he had to see you I give in and tracked you."

Ames winced. If one man could track him in this wilderness, especially when he'd taken such pains to leave no sign, then another could.

"What's this all about?" he asked, slowly accepting the extended hand of Captain Will Kirk. "You in the Army?"

Kirk shook his head. "Nope. Arizona Rangers. I'm here to—" He stopped abruptly as Ames stepped back, his hand hovering over the butt of his Colt. "Hold up, son," the other said quickly. "This is a peaceable mission."

"I reckon I better wait down by the creek," Hammicker said and moved away, dragging his horse after him.

"Let's set," Kirk said and dropped to the ground in a sitting position, his hands resting on his knees. "Might as well be comfortable while I get a load off my chest."

Ames felt a crackle of excitement run through him. He'd heard that the Arizona Rangers were being formed, patterned much after the Texas Rangers of the Lone Star State. He seated himself beside the ranger captain and waited patiently.

Captain Kirk reached inside his coat and brought out a folded sheet of paper. "What I got here is amnesty for one Richard Ames," he said. "That's you, I reckon?"

Ames nodded.

"Amnesty means that there's no longer anything hanging over your head."

"I know what it means," Ames said bleakly.

Kirk smiled. "Yes. You would know. Well, this piece of paper is signed by the Governor and it's as legal as the Constitution."

"What do I have to do to get it?"

"Naturally, there are conditions. I suppose you know this country is havin' growing pains. But we're still kind of spread out and there's a hell of a lot of bad men among all the good ones."

"Some people consider me among the bad ones," Ames said.

"A few do, yes. But I know different. You've done a lot of good in your time, Ames. I've heard a lot of the stories and I checked some of them out—enough to know how you've been occupying your time for the past dozen years."

41

"How'd you know where to find me?"

Kirk chuckled. "Young lad up in Colorado named Halstead. He didn't want to give you away at first. But when I showed him this amnesty paper he come through in a hurry."

"What is it you want me to do?"

"Join the Rangers."

Ames was silent for a long time. Finally Kirk said, "Your grandfather, Caleb Ames, was a lawman in Texas, Ames."

"So I've heard."

"Your grandpa stood for law and order in Texas. You can do the same thing for Arizona. We're going through now what Texas went through then. You can make a big contribution to this country, Ames. Don't you want to do it?"

"I don't know. For the past dozen years, as you say, I've done a lot of riding. Seems like wherever I go there's trouble. No matter what I do I'm pulled into it. When I see something that should be done I have a crazy kind of urge to do something about it."

"So you agree?"

"I didn't say that. It's one thing to do what I can to help a man or woman or town. I'm a free agent, sort of." He thought of the men he'd faced from behind a blazing gun and they stretched out behind him through the years. He was only thirty-two years old, but suddenly he felt as if he were a hundred years older than hat.

"Wearin' a badge adds to a good man's strength," Kirk pointed out.

"Maybe." Ames' thoughts flashed back over the years, when he'd taken the law into his own hands, usually in the absence of any other law. How would he have felt if he'd worn a badge? Would it have made him stronger? He looked at Kirk.

"I need some time to think about it," he said.

Kirk rose to his feet and dusted his seat. "If that's the way it is," he said gruffly, not able to hide his disappointment.

"Wait. You must have something important you want me to do, or you wouldn't have gone to the trouble of getting those amnesty papers."

Kirk nodded. "There is a serious situation right here in the basin," he said. "There's a man here named Gorton who is one of the most dangerous criminals I've ever known. He's in everything crooked right up to his gizzard."

"Why don't you arrest him?"

"Because I can't prove a thing against him," Kirk said bluntly. "He's a slick one, Ames. He's beyond the law right now, but working in the Basin and knowing it as you do, you can get the deadwood on him."

Ames laughed without humor. "Just like that, huh?"

Kirk mounted his horse. "I'll be in Shelby for a few days. Let me hear as soon as you can. I'll appreciate it." He called out, "Herman, I'm ready to go back to town."

Hammicker rode out of the brush. "All right, Cap'n. I'm ready, too."

Ames looked from Kirk to the old trapper. "A couple of riders trailed you here," he said quietly. "If I were you I'd go back a different way."

"Slade Gorton's men most likely," Kirk said, without astonishment. "Thanks, Arizona."

43

# VI

From his cover, Arizona Ames watched the two riders trailing Kirk and Hammicker. They knew their business. That much was evident to Ames.

Even though Kirk and Hammicker had tried to circle them they had not been successful. Ames quickly saddled Cappy and rode down the trail. He'd assumed that the two gunmen were after Kirk. But when Kirk and Hammicker split up to throw the cautiously advancing strangers off their trail the pair unhesitatingly followed Hammicker.

The strange calvalcade proceeded back toward Shelby, led by Hammicker, who was trailed by the persistent gunmen, all of them under Ames' watchful eye.

Darkness settled down as Ames rode the lonely trail. The moon, he knew, would not rise until late. From the dark shadows he relentlessly trailed the two strangers. His woodsman's instinct enabled him to stay within sight of them and yet remain unheard and unseen.

At the edge of town he pulled up. Hammicker had disappeared and the two strangers sat their horses in the middle of the wide dark street, evidently at loss as to how to proceed. The dim yellow lights of the saloon and tavern spilled out into the dust.

After a moment the two riders moved toward the saloon and dismounted, tied their horses and entered the building.

Ames tied his own horse a few yards beyond and strolled into the saloon. It was half-filled with riders drinking and playing cards. The two strangers stood at the bar just raising their glasses of whisky. Han micker was standing at the end of the bar. He'd just finished his drink, and it was plain to Ames that he had not recognized the two men trailing him.

Ames moved quetly behind a card table, in the shadows. The two men wore rough clothing and had not shaved for some time. They appeared to be professional gunfighters. Ames watched them as they moved up beside Hammicker, a man on each side of him. One of the men had a derringer pressed against Hammicker's back. They were grinning at the old trapper and both of them were talking in low voices. None of the men in the saloon appeared to notice what was going on except the bartender. He simply ignored it.

The three of them pulled away from the bar and started walking in single file toward the door, with Hammicker still in the middle.

-They were almost to the door when Ames moved out of the shadow and into the light. "Stop right there," he said, his voice rising above the idle talk and scrape of feet and chairs.

Silence came down on the saloon and all three men halted.

"Throw that little gun on the floor!" Ames ordered. The man hesitated, then looked over his shoulder. The instant he saw the gun in Ames' hand he hastily threw the derringer down.

By this time everyone in the room was standing. It had happened so fast no one had a chance to grasp what was going on.

"Now walk over to the bar."

"They're Gorton's men," someone muttered.

The two men faded away from Ames, and walked, stiff-legged, to the bar. Ames motioned Hammicker to go outside. He catfooted across the room, keeping

45

the two gunmen covered. He went through the door like a wraith.

A babble of voices welled up in the saloon as the door swung shut on Arizona Ames.

"You'd better get your horse and come with me," Ames said.

Herman nodded and ran toward his horse. Ames keeping an eye on the saloon door, untied Cappy and the two of them swung down the street. In a few minutes they were out of town.

Ames pulled up once and listened for sounds of pursuit and heard nothing. They rode on.

"I'm sure sorry you had to make a play," Hammicker said, after a while. "But I'm glad you was there to do it. I know you wanted to keep it quiet about bein' back here."

"I don't think anybody recognized me," Ames said.

"Gorton's goin' to be hot after you now. Them fellers worked for him. They been trailin' me for a long spell." He was silent a moment and then added: "Even before the Injuns took me."

"Why would they do that?"

Hammicker chuckled. "Because they think I made a big gold strike. They aimed to rob me. That's why."

"You're a trapper, aren't you?"

"That's right. But they thought I was a prospector. Where you takin' me, Arizona?"

"To an old prospector's cabin. Cappy Tanner. He was a friend of mine."

"Yeah, I remember. I been hearin' a lot of talk around town, Arizona, real bad talk. Remember that damn sheriff, the one who jumped us the day we hit town. He's Gorton's man pure and simple. Gorton's

46

got everything tied up, and people are afraid to buck him.''

It all followed a pattern that was familiar, Ames thought gloomily. ''You hear anything about the Playfords?''

''Gawd, yes. The talk is Gorton's got him all sewed up one way or another. Say, pard, I'm awful tired. Reckon I'm gettin' old.''

''We'll pull off the trail and camp for the rest of the night,'' Ames said. ''No hurry, old timer.''

They turned off the trail and rode a short distance and dismounted. Without making a fire they rolled in their blankets and were soon asleep.

Ames awoke to the raucous calls of an early-visiting jay. He lay in his blanket for a few minutes as the inquisitive bird called from a nearby tree. Then he rolled out and built a small fire. By the time Herman sat up, yawning, Ames had coffee, bacon and bread ready.

After a quick breakfast they saddled and rode on toward Cappy Tanner's hidden canyon. As they rode Hammicker talked endlessy of doings in town, not failing to mention that he'd seen Mescal and Manzanita, Ames' young sisters. ''They sure are pretty lil' things,'' Herman said.

They came up the valley under Mescal Ridge, and Ames felt a strange sense of nostalgia when he caught a glimpse of the Ames cabin through the trees. They rode past and soon came into the side canyon where Cappy Tanner's place was located.

A tall black horse whinnied as they rode up. The animal was tied to a tree. As Arizona Ames stepped down from the saddle the door burst open and a black-haired girl plunged out, screaming, with Slade Gor-

47

ton's hand on her shoulder, trying to stop her. Her blouse had been almost ripped away, and her half-exposed bosom gleamed whitely through the rents.

Ames hurled across the intervening space, and chopped squarely at Gorton's arm, breaking the man's hold. He felt the old burning rage fly up in him. But his hand didn't go to the gun on his belt. His only thought was to beat Gorton senseless.

He sent his fist crashing into Gorton's face, dropping him. Gorton just sat on the ground for a moment, his eyes glazed, blood dribbling from his nose. Then with a curse, Gorton heaved himself up and rushed at Ames with his fists flying. His sudden recovery took Ames by surprise, and the savage rush carried both men into the brush.

Ames tripped over a dead branch and went down with Gorton's hands encircling his neck. Gorton tried to knee him and got in a painful kick before Ames struggled to his feet and flung he other's arms aside, breaking his hold.

He stepped aside, avoiding Gorton's second rush and started slugging him with right and left jabs to the jaw. With a hoarse cry Gorton went down on his knees, grabbed up the branch Ames had tripped over and swung it with a savage twist to his standing opponent's face. Ames brushed the branch aside, then grabbed hold of it and used it to send Gorton toppling backwards before he could let go of it.

The reverse leverage not only sent Slade Gorton sprawling it filled him with a beaten man's despairing rage and made him reach for his gun.

Ames hit him a solid blow that had the sound of a board slapping a horse's flank. Gorton gasped, his eyes rolled and he flattened out on the ground.

48

Ames waited a moment but the man didn't move.

"Gawd almighty," Hammicker exclaimed. "You hit him a good one, Arizona."

Ames looked at the girl. She was cowering against the wall, trying to cover the rents in her blouse.

"You go on in the house and fix up, Miss," Ames drawled. "That desert weasel inside a human-looking pelt won't bother you again." He patted the weeping girl's shoulder. She almost fell against him, resting her head on his chest.

"Not while Ari—I mean not whilst my friend is around," Hammicker added grimly.

"My—my husband is away," the girl sobbed. "If Ted were here he'd never have dared try what he did. Oh, I hate that man! He's been bothering me ever since Ted and I moved in here."

"This is Cappy Tanner's plac," Ames said.

"Yes. He left it to Ted before he died. I'm Janetta, Ted's wife." She stepped back from Ames in confusion.

"Well, this is Herman Hammicker," Ames said.

"Please excuse me," Janetta said hurriedly, before the old trapper could acknowledge the introduction. She hastily disappeared into the cabin.

"Lord, she's sure's a good looker!" Hammicker exclaimed.

Gorton began to stir and Ames went over and pulled him to his feet. "Get on your horse and don't come back!" Ames said. "I catch you up here again, and there'll be gunplay, Gorton."

Gorton climbed groggily into the saddle. He sat there for a moment, swaying. Then his face cleared and he glowered at Arizona Ames. His eyes hooded and he nodded. "There'll be gunplay anyhow," he

49

said thickly and jabbed spurs to the high spirited black horse. The animal bounded away.

"He plumb forgot his hat," Hammicker said, picking up an expensive black Stetson. "Sure is a fine one."

At a sudden clatter of hooves Ames whirled, drawing his gun. He slowly thrust it back in leather when a young man rode in on a gaunt buckskin and dismounted. He was dark-haired and dark-eyed and there were worry lines on his smooth face. He was dressed in worn jeans, scuffed boots and a ragged brush jacket. He looked at the house and then at Ames and Hammicker.

"Why did Slade Gorton go bustin' out of here like that?" he demanded. "What's goin' on here? And just who are you?"

Neither Ames or Hammicker answered at once, and the young man went on, "I'm Ted Sullivan. This is my—" He stopped speaking as the cabin door flew open, and Janetta dashed out, and across the ground into his arms.

"Thank God, you're all right," Sullivan muttered, patting his wife on her shoulder. "What is this all about?"

In a broken voice, Janetta told him how Slade Gorton had tried to attack her. Ted Sullivan listened in tight-lipped silence. Then he strode to Ames and put out his hand. "I can't tell you how grateful I am," he said. "I been breakin' horses for Slink Tate," Sullivan added. "Been there about a week, I reckon. But I'm behaving like one hell of a homesteader, letting guests I'm beholden to stand around without inviting them inside. You hungry?"

"Tolerable."

"Well, Janetta can remedy that. She's not only the best-lookin' girl in the basin, but she's a real fine cook, if I do say it myself." He took a package out from under his brush jacket, blushing as he did so. "I brought her a little present," he said.

"You go on ahead and give it to her," Ames said. "We need a little more time to rest up. It was pretty strenuous here, just before you arrived."

Ames and Hammicker lounged on the bench in front of the cabin and tried not to listen to the voices inside. Ames felt an ache in his heart every time he ecountered a man and woman in love. It carried him straight back to the day in Colorado when Esther had been taken from him.

"They're a mighty fechin' pair," Herman said, in a low voice. "Reckon they're just plumb crazy about each other, Ames."

"Huh? Oh, sure. I was thinking of something else."

"You must have been. There was a funny expression on your face, but maybe funny ain't the word for it."

"It was anything but funny," Ames said.

There was a shy laugh and the sound of a kiss and Ted Sullivan came out of the cabin, a bemused expression on his face. He glanced guiltily at Ames and Hammicker and settled himself on the bench besides Ames.

"How did you come by this cabin?" Ames asked.

"Well, an old trapper named Cappy Tanner willed it to me and Janetta took care of him when he was dying. We like it here. It's quiet and peaceful, and I've never cared much for town living. Janetta worked in a dance hall before we were married and that may be one reason Gorton has been after her the way he has. You know what lies people tell about dance hall girls.''

His eyes flashed. ''I'm not much of a hand with a gun. But Gorton had better not come back here again, if he wants to stay alive.''

''You said something about breaking horses for Slink Tate?''

Sullivan nodded. ''Slink's not a bad sort. He's all crippled up from a gunfight he had a number of years ago with a young helion named Arizona Ames.'' Ted Sullivan's voice deepened with admiration. ''It's kind of a legend around here—the way Arizona Ames shot it out with a crooked sheriff and then two Tates. He killed one Tate, and the sheriff, and shot Slink up so bad he has never been the same since.''

It was strange, Arizona thought, hearing an experience he'd lived through being retold by a young stranger who had no idea the man he was talking about was sitting right beside him. His attention came back to young Sullivan as the boy went on admiringly:

''Guess Ames had to run for it, because killing that no-good sheriff was a pretty serious thing. The stories about him that have drifted back have made some people feel he's turned gun-slinging wild. But I've never believed—'' He broke off, staring. ''Don't tell me you ain't heard of the famous Arizona Ames?''

Ames nodded. ''I've heard of him,'' he said quietly, a pleasant smile on his tanned face.

''What do you know about Slade Gorton?'' Ames asked, after a pause.

Ted Sullivan shook his head. ''Nobody knows much about where he's from,'' he said. ''He just showed up here between two days some time ago. He dresses like a dandy but he's a dangerous man. He singled out

52

our big rancher in these parts, Sam Playford. Playford's married to Nesta Ames, Arizona's sister. They've got a fine boy named Rich—after Arizona.''

Ames found himself wondering if young Sullivan knew that Nesta had been a wild, wilful and beautiful girl and that it had been really her fatal attraction for one of the Tates that had led him into the gunfight that had branded him an outlaw.

"Gorton made up to Playford," Sullivan went on. "They seemed thick as thieves. But Sam Playford seemed to go into a shell about that time. He was always a real happy man but all of a sudden, he changed, and became gloomy as all get-out. He dropped all of his old friends, and developed a yard-wide suspicious streak.

"But to get back to Gorton. He got his own man put in charge of the Indian Agency and he's stealing the Apache blind. One of these days they're goin' to break out.''

"Some of them already broke out," Hammicker said fervently. "I know!''

Sullivan looked at him curiously for a moment and then went on: "Slade sells whisky and guns to renegades. It's suspected by some that he might be one of the Wild Bunch!''

"No!'' Herman ejaculated.

Sullivan nodded vigorously. "It wouldn't surprise me too much if he turned out to be Butch Cassidy himself!''

"That can't be,'' Hammicker said. "I saw Cassidy once—and he don't look nothin' like Gorton.''

"Well, Lay then, or maybe that other one—the cool one that liked to kill.''

"That's what broke 'em up,'' Herman said. "I

mean Cassidy just wouldn't tolerate a cold-blooded killer, much of an outlaw as he is.''

"It's possible," Ames admitted, although he seriously doubted that Gorton had ever ridden with the Wild Bunch.

Their discussion ended when Janetta Sullivan announced from the cabin doorway, "Dinner's on the table. Come and get it before it turns ice-cold.''

Sunset gilded the Mazatals when they trooped into the cabin. In the doorway, Ames lifted his eyes to the lofty walls, cragged and ledged, shining in the golden light, and the yawning black gulf of timber with which the canyon was choked. He experienced once again a stirring of the old feelings he'd had for this Basin. It was and always would be his home.

They seated themselves at the table Ames remembered, and Janetta placed steaming pans before them. Good as the food was, the interest of everybody centered on getting the meal over, and conversation ceased to be their main concern. The clearing off of the table was accomplished with quick dispatch while the men smoked and talked.

Finally, Arizona Ames rose, stretching to his full height. "Herman, I think it's about time we hit the trail,'' he said.

"You can stay here," Ted Sullivan said quickly. "You can sleep in the loft. It isn't much but it's better than ridin' the trail back to Shelby this time of night.''

And so it was that Ames found himself, after climbing the steep ladder leading into the loft, as Sullivan called it, reclining stretched out at full length on a soft feather tick on a big brass bed. Herman, scorning a bed, rolled himself in a blanket on the floor and soon began snoring.

54

Ames did not fall asleep at once. The branches of spruce and maple that overgrew the cabin brushed against the roof and the leaves rustled. The wind under the eaves had a wailing note. It brought to Ames more than the meaning of a fall breeze.

There was deep trouble in Tonto Basin. It was up to him to settle the matter.

In the old days he would have agonized about it and made a decision, which would usually end in a gunfight. Now he had the added pressure from Captain Kirk of the Arizona Rangers. The ranger chief had not implied that the amnesty was conditional on Ames' becoming a Ranger. But Ames shrewdly figured that such might be the case. And that was unfortunate, for he had just about decided he did not want to be a man bound by the rigors of an officially disciplined way of life.

He turned restlessly in his bed and at long last, after the poignant murmuring voices in the cabin below were silenced, he slept.

## VII

Even a half dozen years before, nothing much had mattered to Arizona Ames. Everything except death had happened to him—love, anguish, happiness, all of it. That love itself had escaped him just as he had begun to experience it in all of its richness and depth had left him embittered beyond recall—or so he'd thought.

And yet he awoke on this morning with a growing pleasure and a growing awareness that he was living again.

"You look kinder wild, but you ain't drunk," Ham-

55

micker said from his blanket on the floor. "You ain't had nothin' that I know about."

"I'm feeling my oats, Herman," Ames said and came out of the old brass bedstead to begin dressing. "All of a sudden everything seems as if it's going to be all right."

"Wal, that young couple down there might have somethin' to do with it, Ames. There ain't nothin' like young'uns to make the whole dad-burned world light up again!"

Ames brought up an answer only to have it cut short by the sudden shout of a piercing scream.

"What the hell?" exclaimed Hammicker.

He got no answer from Ames who swung easily down through the trapdoor and dropped to the floor of the cabin.

Janetta Sullivan was crouched in a corner, her eyes wide and frightened. She was trembling like a leaf in a wind. Sullivan stood back from her, his back bowed. He held a heavy revolver in his hand.

Both of them appeared unhurt to Ames. He went forward until he was between Sullivan and his wife. He leaned down to take Janetta's hand and found it cold.

"What's going on here?" he asked softly.

"She tried to kill herself!" Sullivan said bluntly. "I woke up and saw her with this gun to her temple and the hammer back. I got it away from her just in time!"

"Why?" Ames asked in a grim voice.

Janetta withdrew her hand from his and looked at him with unfathomable eyes. Her hand shook, her full bosom rose and fell, and her lips were set in a bitter line.

"Well, why?" Ames asked again.

Sullivan answered for her in a broken voice: "Yesterday wasn't the first day Gorton's been here. He came before. And it seems he got what he come for. That's what she finally confessed to me, after I took this gun away from her!"

"I wronged Ted," Janetta said brokenly. "I shamed him."

"Killing yourself wouldn't have helped none," Ames declared. "No matter what happened."

"I'll find a way to finish the job," she whispered. "I can't go on living—"

Ted Sullivan cried out in agonized protest. He dropped the pistol and brushed past Ames to kneel beside his wife. He took her hand and said, "No matter what happened, I love you, Janetta."

"You see how he feels," Ames said.

"Poor Ted." She lifted a hand and touched his face. "I meant what I said, I just can't go on livin'—"

"You can! Don't talk like that," Sullivan said desperately. He turned his head and looked at Ames. His eyes were wild, his face haggard. "You tell her, mister. Please. Make her understand. After what you did yesterday, I feel as if I'd known you all my life. I trust you—"

"It will be better if we just let her talk," Ames said softly. "Go on, Janetta."

"He has come before. He used to stay hidden, and wait for Ted to leave. Then he'd come in, leading his big black horse and dressed like the dandy he is. He tried to bring me presents. He tried to make love to me. I kept him from doing that . . . as long as I could. Then one day he lost control. He grabbed me and ripped my clothes off. He had his way—" She broke down and put her face in her hands and sobbed violently.

Young Ted Sullivan rose, his face working in a mask of hate. He walked past Ames, leaned down and picked up the heavy gun. He stuck it into his belt. "I reckon I know what I've got to do," he said.

Ames spun him around. "You don't have to do anything," he said in a steely voice. "You leave this to me. Your place is here with your wife."

Young Sullivan put his head against the cabin wall and began to sob, his shoulders shaking. When he turned back to face Ames again there was a look of grim determination in his eyes. "It's up to me," he said, hardly able to speak.

"I said I'd take care of it," Ames said. "You and Janetta just go on like you've been, and try to forget this ever happened." He noticed Herman Hammicker then. The old man had hurriedly dressed and came down the ladder into the room.

"Let's go, Herman," Ames said.

Hammicker followed him out of the cabin. They caught up their horses and saddled and rode toward Shelby.

"What you goin' to do, Ames?" Hammicker asked uneasily, when they were on the trail.

"Repeat what I've done before," said Ames.

He looked at the distant ridges with a far-seeing eye, feeling the beauty of the morning but not actually seeing it. He was plunged into the past, on the day that his sister Nesta had tried to kill herself on her wedding day because of Lee Tate. That was the day that he'd killed the sheriff, and Lee Tate who'd taken his sister Nesta by force. That was the day he'd become a fugitive and begun his wanderings.

He told Hammicker all about that day, finding a release in the telling.

And now it's goin' to start all over again," he said in a hoarse voice. "I'm going to kill Slade Gorton. I'm going to call him out, Herman."

"Son, you can't do that," Herman said earnestly. "Things ain't like they used to be."

"You tell me how it is, Herman," Ames said. "That's how it's been with me for years. There was Rankin the rustler and no way for the law to touch him. Yes, and Crow Crieve, the wife-beatin' rancher. And some others."

"Arizona, I ain't denyin' you done what had to be done. But you can't go this route now. Not the day after Cap'n Kirk talked to you about law and order."

"You listened," said Ames, accusingly.

"No, I didn't," Hammicker said with dignity. "Cap'n Kirk talked to me about what he was goin' to tell you." He glanced at Ames. "Do we have to quarrel, Arizona? Is it necessary?"

Ames chuckled despite his feelings. "I reckon we don't, old timer. What do you suggest I do? Join the Rangers?"

"You could do worse," Hammicker told him.

Leaving Hammicker to take care of the horses, Ames walked to the hotel to find Captain Kirk. He was reliving the day when he was just past eighteen and in his first gunfight. He kept remembering how Lee Tate had looked as he lay dying. Ames shook his head. He didn't want that to happen again.

Kirk wasn't in his room and Ames returned to the street, wondering where he might find the Ranger chief. He looked up and down the street which was near empty and didn't catch sight of the tall Ranger.

59

He strolled back toward the livery where he'd left Hammicker.

The sound of voices reached him as he neared the big double-doored entryway. The mean edge of the voices brought him around to the side of the barn and toward the corral at the rear. He cornered the back side of the barn and stopped short at the sight that met his eyes. Herman was backed against the barn with the two rough riders facing him, their attitude threatening. As Ames watched one of the men slapped Herman across the face.

"C'mon, old man, we ain't got all day. Tell us where you got that gold cashed out."

"I ain't got no gold," Herman protested. Ames could see he'd been hit before, because blood was dripping from his nostrils.

The man struck him again, this time with his balled fist. Herman stumbled back against the barn.

"Hold it right there," Ames said in a soft and deadly voice.

The two men whirled and both started their draw, just as some town people, hearing the noise rounded the opposite corner from Ames.

Ames made his draw with an automatic, precise flash and two shots boomed out before the guns of the two men facing him were clear of their holsters. One of the men screamed, and clutched at his chest. The other crumpled backward, slowly, as though he were simply settling down for a nap.

"Good God!" a man said in an awed voice. "Arizona Ames has done come back!"

Ames looked down at his gun, and the thin ribbon of smoke that was still coming from the barrel. Slowly, and with a steady hand he shoved out two empties,

60

reloaded the pistol and sheathed it. He looked at Hammicker, and said in a dead voice, "Come on, Herman, let's get out of here."

## VIII

The news went like wildfire through the Tonto Basin that Arizona Ames had returned.

On the small ranches in the sheltered valleys it was talked about over the supper table, in the yellow light of kerosene lamps, where the smell of cooking and coffee and the rattle of plates and cutlery were part of the talk.

The valley of the Tonto was full of golden light. The sun had just set behind the bold brow of Mescal Ridge, and a wonderful flare of gold, thrown up against a dark bank of purple cloud, seemed to be reflected down the valley.

Arizon Ames sat his horse above the creek, where many a time he had rested before, and watched the magic glow on field and slope and water. Already the air had begun to cool, and the gold swept by as if it had been the transparent shadow of a cloud, swift and evanescent, like a dream, or a fleeting happiness.

Wild ducks went whirring down the creek, the white bars on their wings twinkling. A big buck, his coat the gray-blue of fall, crossed an opening in the brush. Up high somewhere an old gobbler was calling his flock to roost.

"Sure is pretty, ain't it?" Herman Hammicker said.

Ames sighed, a deep sigh, for al the good things he'd missed in the passing years. Here lay the place he'd wanted to be all that time. Now he was home

61

again and it seemed as if all the troubles of all the years he'd been away piling up once more.

"Yes. I wouldn't exchange this for any other land-fall and I've seen a lot of them in my thirty-odd years."

"Then why you so dad-gummed black-browed?'

"It's the same old thing," Ames said gloomily. "I guess I better get on down to Sam and Nesta's place. The word is out I'm back and I don't want them to find out from anybody but me."

Their horses picked the way carefully down toward what had been Sam Playford's homestead in the dim, distant past. Now it was all changed, Ames saw, as they emerged from the timber into the valley proper. Herds of cattle grazed in the evening shadows as they rode toward the distant ranch house.

Playford had become a big man in Tonto. His holdings ran into thousands of acres, and his cattle dotted the valley slopes and level grazing lands for miles. Ames remembered him as a big, homely man with clear gray eyes, wearing plain homesteaders' jeans.

As Playford came out of the house Ames could see at a glance that he'd changed. He held himself just as straight and he had the same clear, gray eyes. But now they seemed sunken and haunted.

It was Nesta that took his eye as he dismounted. She knew him at once and flew into his arms. He remembered her as she'd been on the day he'd dragged her from the creek, and what a transformation had taken place. She'd been a slender, pale-faced girl, pretty of course. But now she was tall, full-bosomed, and as beautiful as one of the golden flowers of the valley.

"Rich!" she said in a choked voice. "I knew you'd come back some day."

The old petulance, wildness and the girlishness were gone. He could sense it as her warmth invaded him. He stood back from her and looked in her eyes which were now swimming with tears.

"Well, now, you haven't changed a bit!"

"Rich Ames, you were always an awful liar!" she exclaimed, drawing him toward the Porch. "Sam, aren't you going to say a word?"

Sam Playford gripped Ames' hand. "Shore glad you're home," he said in a voice devoid of feeling.

Ames exchanged glances with his sister and she shook her head.

Nesta talked on, fast, as though to forestall any unpleasantness. "We were almost ready to sit down to supper," she said. "Sam, why don't you show Rich around until I ring the bell."

"Where's my young namesake?" Ames asked afer introducing Herman.

"Young Rich? He's off hunting somewhere," Nesta said, sighing. "He's just like you were, Rich. Always prowling the wild country. With a gun, of course." She gave him and Playford a shove. "Get along with you both. Herman, you can come on in and fill the lamps for me."

Herman complied with alacrity and Playford and Ames walked toward the big barn with its corral filled with sleek riding horses. "Sam, you've done real well," Ames said, as they stopped to watch the colorful sunset.

"Yeah, I reckon."

"All those cabins down there—" Ames pointed to the row of small cabins reaching away from the ranch.

"Well, you wrote Nesta about the Grieve ranch up in Wyoming," Playford said. "We patterned it after

63

that, Rich. Two men in a cabin. The cabins are nice, with their own fireplace and runnin' water. There ain't a cowboy in the whole Southwest wouldn't come work here, if he had the chance.''

"Well, I'm forgetful, kind of. Seems to me when I left here you were about the happiest man I ever laid eyes on. What's gnawing on you, Sam?''

Playford gave him a weak smile. "Nothing, Rich. I swear it.''

Ames started to tell Sam about the letter from Nesta, but decided against it. He walked with Playford as the big man, with occasional flashes of pride, talked about how he had built the Playford spread up into the imposing holding it had become. "Reckon if it hadn't been for your sister I never would have made it," he said, and for a moment his voice no longer seemed cold and distant.

"Well, you've still got your wife and a fine boy," Ames pointed out. "If there is something amiss here, Sam, you'd better handle it just like you've handled everything else—up to now, that is.''

Playford turned a haggard face on Ames. In the twilight his features twitched. He opened his mouth and then closed it again. He turned and said tonelessly, "We better get back. Supper's 'most ready.''

Ames felt a stinging disappointment. He had the feeling that Playford had been on the point of speaking out. He forced himself to be patient. Playford was clearly a man who had almost reached the breaking point. Before he broke, Sam Playford would talk and then it would all come pouring out.

When Ames and Playford reached the ranch house, they discovered that Nesta had sent a cowboy with a

64

buckboard to the old place and fetched Mrs. Ames and the twins.

The two girls, Manzi and Mescal, descended on Ames with squeals of delight, smothering him with hugs and kisses. After a while he drew back, gasping.

"Good grief," he said gravely, "I knew you two had grown up, but you're behaving like you did when Cappy used to bounce you on his knee, or let you ride piggy-back on his shoulders around the cabin."

The girls instantly became prim, young ladies, looking demurely down, only the mischievous glint of their eyes betraying their excitement.

Mescal tossed her head. "It's hard to believe my own brother would ask me the direction to Uncle Cap's old place, and not tell me who he was."

Manzi drew herself up proudly. "I knew who he was, all the time."

"Oh, you didn't either!" Mescal said in mock anger. "You'd have told me if you had known."

"But I did, I tell you. He rode off straight as an arrow. I told him to go by our place to get there. But I was. So I knew he'd just asked us a question because he wanted to talk to us!"

"Well, that much is true," said Ames.

"You all set up to the table," Nesta directed. The twins quarreled about who would have the place next to Ames, and Mrs. Ames settled it by placing one on each side of him, and moving him down from the foot of the table.

Sam Playford was relaxed for once. He seemed to rejoice in the fact that all the remaining members of the family were gathered under his roof. Perhaps, Ames thought, somewhere in Playford's mind there gleamed a faint hope that his return might bring about a change in circumstances which, in some way, were making it impossible for him to remain the kind of man that Nesta had married. Nesta looked at her husband with a happy light in her blue eyes.

And then she looked at the prodigal brother who was responsible for a lightening of all their spirits.

Young Rich was silent, never taking his eyes from his famous uncle all through the meal. He scarcely touched his food, he was so excited. He listened to the grown-up talk and dreamed his own dreams.

Herman noticed the boy's admiring, almost worshipful gaze and chuckled quietly. "Me and Rich, here," he said, placing a gnarled hand on the boy's shoulder, "we're old trapping pardners."

"I'm going to show Uncle Herman where all the fur game is," Rich said shyly. He looked expectantly at Ames and added: "I know this Basin better than anybody."

"I'll bet you do," said Ames. He sat there in a glow, listenin to a conversation that revolved almost entirely about the people he'd known in his own youth. It all brought back vivid—and sometimes painful—memories.

After supper Ames gazed around the big living room, utterly happy to be with his family once more. Beside more than one lonely campfire in his wandering he'd dreamed of this day and until it actually happened he had thought it never would come about.

At last it was time to go. It was decided that Ames and Hammicker would occupy one of the cabins down by the creek. Nesta followed him out and they stood in the cool night while Herman made his way through the darkness.

Nesta squeezed Ames' arm. "Oh, Rich, what a joy it is that you came."

"I couldn't do anything else after I got your letter."

"I didn't dare hope you would. I prayed night and morning. But I can tell you've had more than your share of troubles. There's a sadness in your eyes that makes my heart bleed." She stared up at him in the darkness. "You've never found a girl to love?"

Ames remained silent for a moment, while a tormenting memory came back into his mind. "There was a girl up in Colorado," he said at last. "She was killed the day we were to be married."

"Oh, Rich!" Nesta breathed. "I'm so sorry."

Realizing that she was crying, he put his arm around her shoulder. "I'm trying to forget," he said simply. "Now tell me about Sam."

"There's nothing more I can tell you about Sam," she said. "Ever since Slade Gorton come to town Sam's been a changed man. I don't know what hold he has over Sam, but it's something evil. I can't get a thing out of him no matter how hard I try."

"I keep thinking that the only way to take care of this is to take care of Gorton," Ames said slowly, with a tightening in his chest that was almost painful.

Nesta laid a trembling head on his arm. "That mustn't happen again. Not here, not in the old way."

"Things are different and yet they're the same," Ames said, Bitterly. "I ran into some of Gorton's work up at Uncle Cappy's old place. Gorton raped Janetta Sullivan."

Nesta gasped. "Oh, God, Rich—I knew he was an evil man but to do something like that. And Janetta—She was a dancehall girl, but she is just as good as she's beautiful."

67

"I figured as much," said Ames. "Well, you run off to bed now. I need a good night's rest." He stopped speaking and suddenly grabbed his sister and fell to the ground with her as a muzzle flash erupted a few feet from where they had been standing. The shot rang out like a thunderpeal when a storm was overhead, almost deafening them.

"Stand right there!" Ames breathed harshly. He ran back to the house, with the pound of a hard-running horse in his ears. He failed to catch a glimpse of the hidden rifleman, nor could he see in which direction the would-be assassin had fled.

Lights were going on all over the ranch. He found Nesta still crouching where he had left her. "Go back to the house," he told her in a low voice. "Tell them I accidentally dropped my gun, and it went off."

Nesta was too badly shaken to say anything in reply. She simply turned, and went stumbling away in the direction of the cabin. Ames walked through the night to the lighted cabin where Herman Hammicker stood in the doorway, looking anxiously out into the darkness.

"Thought I heard a shot," were his first words.

"Old timer, you hear pretty good," Ames said. "Just keep it under your hat. But somebody tried to bushwhack me a minute ago."

"Aw, you're foolin'," said Herman.

"Not a bit of it. Come on, let's get some sleep. We'll take a look in the morning and see what tracks we can find."

## IX

Ames awoke early and went out into the pre-dawn

darkness, leaving Herman Hammicker asleep. He savored the smell of Indian Summer in the cool fresh air as he walked up to the yellow-lighted cook shack. He pushed into the warm air of the shack and said, "You got a cup of coffee for a hungry man?"

"You bet," replied the cook. "You Miz Nesta's brother, ain't you?" He came from the stove wiping his hands on his apron. He stuck out his hand. "We all heard a lot about Arizona Ames."

Ames shook hands with the cook. "How many riders has Sam got?"

"Well, now, we just finished fall roundup and some of them are gone already. We keep about eight steady, year round." He went back to his stove and stirred an enormous pot. His head became obscured for a moment by a cloud of swiftly rising steam. "Mister Playford just paid off the extra hands," he said.

He walked to the door and banged two or three times on the iron triangle outside. "Got to keep down the racket this early in the mawnin'," he said as he came back. "Better stand back if you don't want to get killed in the rush."

The riders stampeded in as though they'd been waiting outside for an hour at least. They stopped their ribald chatter when they caught sight of Ames.

"Boys, this here is Arizona Ames," the cook said. "He's goin' to join you-all fur breakfass this mawnin'."

The riders mumbled their howdys, and scrambled into seats around the table. At least half of them looked at him in awe, the rest looked startled and respectful.

"Arizona, I put an extra plate down at the end 'specially for you," the cook said. "Just push the hawgs out of the way and set yourself down."

Ames took his seat where the cook had indicated

69

and began eating a steaming bowl of cereal. This was followed with biscuits, eggs and bacon and the only sounds were those of hungry cowhands eating.

After breakfast, Ames followed the riders outside and watched them saddle up and start out for their day's work. The foreman, a salty cowpuncher named Lanny Ross, tolled them off, giving them their orders and when the last rider loped away the sun had come up over the rim of the mountains.

Lanny sighed with relief. "It's a chore," he said, "keepin' 'em busy in late fall and winter. But we can't let good men go, else we'd be hurtin' come spring." He squinted at Ames. "You figure to stay long?"

"I don't know," Ames said. "Just looking around right now, taking it easy and in a hurry to go no place."

"Yeah, I see. Anything I can do to help out?"

"You been here long?"

"Close to eight years. There was just me and Sam in the beginnin'. It sort of makes me feel like I helped Sam build all this."

"You've every right to feel that way. How does Sam get along with the Tates?"

"Well, you know there's just one of them left. That's old Slink and he ain't much good no more. All crippled up. He don't give us no trouble."

"What is bothering Sam?"

Lanny Ross bent piercing gray eyes on Ames. "Reckon Slade Gorton's back of all our trouble. Leastwise, it all started happenin' after he showed up."

"You know what Gorton's game is?"

Ross shook his head. "But I do know this, Arizona. He's a dangerous man if I ever saw one. A cold killer who'd steal the nickels off his dead grandma's eyes. That's the kind of man he is!"

Herman Hammicker came out of the bunk cabin rubbing his eyes. He sighted Ames and Ross standing there, and came toward them in his woodsman's stride.

"I hope I ain't too late for the food trough," he said.

"Go right on in," Ross said with hospitality. "Cookie always keeps a little somethin' on." He looked at Ames. "If you'll excuse me I have to do a bit of fence mendin'."

Ames led Hammicker into the cook shack and watched him put away a big breakfast. When the last bit of bacon was gone, Hammicker leaned back with a satisfied sigh. "Can't see why anybody'd ever quit this spread," he said belching. "Gives a man what he needs to make him happy in life."

"Why, thank you kindly, sir," the cook spoke up. "That's mighty neighborly of you."

The reputation of Arizona Ames either preceded him wherever he roamed or arrived with him. And it had built in Tonto Basin to a disproportionate degree. Tales had drifted over the West which had given him a reputation that he felt was unjustified. But it was there and he couldn't shut his eyes to it. The more mystery built up like a snowbank about Ames, the more everyone seemed to give him credit for making it happen.

"Herman, let's you and me take a look at some tracks," Ames said.

"Yeah. Let's," Herman agreed and rose and followed Ames outside.

They went up to the ranch house and Ames showed Herman where he'd stood when the hidden gunman had taken a shot at him. Herman went to the spot Ames indicated, and dropped to his hands and knees.

While he looked for only what he could see he sang the saga of Sam Bass:

*"Sam Bass he came from Indiana—it was his native state;*

*He came out here to Texas, and here he met his fate.*

*Sam always drank good liquor and spent his money free,*

*And a kinder-hearted feller you'd seldom ever see!"*

At last Herman rose to his feet. He looked at Ames. "Just one man. He took the one shot and dusted out fast Ames. From what I can figure he headed back toward Shelby."

"Let's get our horses," Ames said bleakly. "Might as well make certain."

"All right. You're the boss."

They saddled their horses and Herman took the lead, riding sign on the faint hoof marks in the dry dust. Every now and then he'd get down from the saddle and carefully scan the ground on his hnds and knees.

While he looked at the tracks he sang:

*"Sam Bass he came from Indiana—it was his native state."*

After awhile Herman stood up and climbed on his horse. "Ain't no question about it, Ames. That bushwhacker headed straight for town."

Ames tossed aside his cigarette, and mounted also. "Let's ride into Shelby, Herman."

"Ames, you ain't goin' in there to pick a fight?"

"No. I'm going to see Kirk. If I can find him."

"Halley-yoo-yer! You're goin' to take that there badge!"

"No, that wasn't my idea exactly," Ames told him.

72

"But there's something important I want to talk to him about."

A cowboy from the Tate spread brought the word to old Sling Tate that Arizona Ames had returned to the Basin.

"He killed two of Gorton's men," the cowboy said. "Shot 'em both before they could get their guns out."

Slink sat with a blanket around his shoulders. His face, like that of a surly hound, had leached out when he became an invalid. His sunken gloomy eyes lifted to the cowhand. There were things he could never forget or forgive and they all revolved about Arizona Ames.

"Send the boys up," he said in a dry and lifeless voice.

The cowboy hurried away to round up the crew.

Anna Belle Tate came into the room and adjusted the blanket around her father's shoulder.

"Who was that?" she asked. She was not a conventionally pretty girl but her face had a striking beauty, somewhat bony and set off by her marvelous purple eyes.

"Arizona Ames is back," he said, still in the same lifeless voice.

"Does it matter?" she asked indifferently.

"He killed Lee." He lifted his gloomy eyes to her for a moment. "He put me in a sick bed for the rest of my life."

"All that is past and done with."

"No. It ain't done with. It won't be done with until he's six feet under."

"All that killing!" she cried. "All to no purpose. It's a sin to take a life—"

73

"Don't go spoutin' that stuff on me," Slink said harshly. "Get out of here, gal. Get out and stay out. The men are comin' and I don't want you to hear what I'm goin' to tell 'em to do."

"What's that?" she cried. "What'll you tell them?"

"To kill Ames. Now, git!"'

Ted Sullivan stopped in Turner's saloon to see if any of the cattlemen were there. He was a horsebreaker and he needed work. He'd broken the green string for Slink Tate and now that he was through with that, there had to be another job and soon.

The only cattleman in the place was old Nelse Hornsby who had a very small spread way up the valley. Ted Sullivan spoke to him and asked him if he'd need any horses broken.

From the vantage point of his office window, Gorton had seen Sullivan ride in and tie his horse and go into Turner's. He sent one of his men around with instruction to plant the idea in Sullivan's mind that there was something going on between Ames and Janetta.

This man, Garth Hedges, a rustler, horsethief and gunman, strolled into the saloon just as Hornsby had informed Sullivan that he didn't have any work for him.

Garth, a handsome, light-haired man with friendly blue eyes, edged up beside Sullivan and said, "Howdy, Ted. How about a drink?"

"I don't drink," Sullivan said. He knew Hedges by reputation and didn't want anything to do with him. Hedges was a persuasive man with the gift of flattery, and in a short time he had Ted Sullivan drinking a sarsparilla. From that it was easy to get him to take a glass of whiskey. At the right moment Hedges let

74

it drop that Arizona Ames was seeing Janetta on the sly.

"That's a downright lie!" Sullivan said angrily. "Ames is my friend! He wouldn't do anything like that. He knocked Gorton to the ground for bothering my wife. He helped me in another way, more than anyone will ever know. And besides that, Janetta wouldn't—"

Hedges laughed knowingly. "Well, ordinarily, sure. But this Arizona Ames is about the most handsome feller around here. And you say he's won your trust. He's the kind that women go crazy about! And if they think their husbands trust a man—" Laughing, he moved away to leave Ted Sullivan to jealous thoughts.

Sullivan forgot about work. He forgot about everything except the attractive features of Arizona Ames, hovering over the receptive friendliness of his wife. He even forgot how many drinks he'd had. But somewhere in the course of a succession of empty glasses he conceived the idea that he had to preserve the honor of his wife. He looked at his gun to see that it was loaded and went out looking for Arizona Ames.

Even if what Hedges had said was true, he doubted if he could ever bring himself to hate Ames the way he hated Gorton for what that filthy beast had done. But the fire of rage that had been lighted by Gorton now was spreading in his tormented, drink-inflamed mind to Ames as well. If Ames, pretending to be his friend, was pursuing with Janetta the same—Oh, God, yes! If that was true, Arizona Ames deserved to die.

# X

It was the strangest of all proposals and Arizona Ames, having found Captain Will Kirk, could not quite believe for a moment that this request would be accepted.

"Just for two weeks, do you understand? If you can deputize me, and pin on an Arizona Ranger badge for just two weeks, I'll do all I can to justify your faith in me. I know now I could never be a Ranger for longer than a couple of weeks. I value my independence too much—the freedom to roam. But if—"

"All right," Kirk had said. "If that's the way you feel—"

From the minute the badge was pinned on, Ames seemed to be a different man. He felt different, in that he sensed the power of the Law behind him. No longer did he feel alone. Captain Kirk had made him realize that operating within the framework of the law would not be to his disadvantage. Quite the contrary.

In his years of wandering Arizona Ames had often found himself involved with people with problems. Invariably it put him behind a smoking gun and he rode away, leaving things better than he had found them through the power and skill of that famed sixgun.

Now the problems were there again and deeply involved were people who meant more to him than anyone else in the world. He realized that he needed the extra power which came from the presence on his chest of a bright silver shield.

Within an hour after his talk with Captain Kirk he learned that Ted Sullivan was looking for him in a drunken rage. He also learned that Slink Tate's cowboys were combing the hidden canyons and valleys looking for him; and all of them were well mounted and heavily armed. Ames' vigilance, not to mention the woodsman's instinct developed during his youthful hunting years, enabled him to cover the Basin undetected. At a safe distance he saw the posse in action, following the lonely search of Ted Sullivan and making contact with those who could tell him of things he could not see for himself.

At noon the following day Ames intercepted Lanny Ross as the foreman rode the trail toward a protected meadow. Ames rode out of a pine thicket and said, "Morning, Lanny. It seems your men are making a roundup. Why at this time of year?"

"We got a contract with the Army to furnish beef for the Indians," Lanny said, squinting at Ames. "You seem to know pretty much everything that's going on."

"I try to get around," Ames conceded.

"Gorton has made the brag that he's goin' to pin that shield on your bare hide," Lanny drawled.

"Frankly, I'm scared to death."

"Yeah, I'll bet. Well, he lost a couple of men but he picked up quite a few more. The bad-actin' kind. I just wish there was somethin' we could do to help. Me, I mean."

"You do help just by talking to me."

"My two-bit talk don't count much, with Gorton and Tate both claimin' they got you on the run."

Ames smiled. Talk was cheap and no one knew that better than he.

Tonto Basin had become a smouldering keg of powder, ready for an explosion at any time.

It's about time something happened, Ames thought, and was not too surprised when, a few minutes after parting with Lanny Ross he caught a glimpse, down

77

through the pines, of a flashy pinto. If he were not mistaken, a woman rode the horse.

The beautiful benchland below was not a long ride from the Tate ranch, and two trails led to it by different routes. Ames had several times seen the brown-and-white pinto but never close at hand.

Ames dismounted and, leading his horse over the soft trail, which gave out no sound, he went on under the pines and through the mahogany brush.

Soon he saw the horse, standing, riderless with but reins down, nipping at grass. He dropped his own reins and went round a corner of green to stop by a huge fallen fir.

Across the log a girl leaned with her back to him. Her hair was dark and the shape of her head was good. She turned, unconscious of his presence, and he was aware that she was a strikingly beautiful woman. Her wide, dark eyes were focused on a nearby bird that sang with a flutter of its throat and a curious tilting of its head from side to side.

A twig snapped under Ames' boot. The girl's head came down quickly. Velvety humid eyes, large and beautiful, stared uncomprehendingly at him.

"You're Arizona Ames?" It was a question and yet a statement.

Ames studied her for a moment, the high lift of her bosom, the sinuous curve of her hip. His gaze went back to her face and her hauntingly beautiful eyes. "I'm Ames," he said.

"Thank Heaven I've found you! I've looked and looked."

"Just why—may I ask?"

"My father and his men are out looking for you. They'll kill you if they find you."

"And you wanted to warn me?"

"Oh, yes," she said breathlessly. "We've had too much violence in the Basin. May father is a harsh, unbending man, and he can't forgive or forget what happened when you—" She looked at him with anxious eyes. "I'm Anna Belle Tate. I am not like my father. I hate violence and cruelty, suffering and death. Someone has to take a stand, and put a stop to it."

"Glad to meet you," Ames said, taking off his hat. "Sorry it's not under—happier circumstances."

"My father gave his men orders not to come back until you are dead."

"Other men have given such orders in the past," Ames smiled. "I'm still alive."

"Oh, but this is different. There are others. Gorton has offered a five thousand-dollar reward for you—dead or alive!" She turned scarlet as she added: "Ted Sullivan has sworn to kill you because of—his wife."

Ames came around the log and seated himself and placed his hat on the ground. He carefully rolled a cigarette and lighted it up.

She threw herself on the ground beside him. "You don't seem very upset about all this."

He shook his head. "I'm mostly pleased, ma'am, that you'd take the trouble to try and warn me."

"I don't want any more bloodshed," she said. "If you just go away it would all end."

"No it wouldn't," Ames told her. "I came back because my sister, Nesta, asked me to. She asked me because her husband is in deep trouble with Slade Gorton."

She shuddered at the mention of Gorton's name. "He's a beast! The worst man I've ever run across!"

79

Impulsively, she placed a hand on Ames' arm. "You can't beat him! He's too powerful, he has too many men. And everything else is working against you. My own father—and Ted Sullivan."

Ames kept silent as she talked. What he felt most was a sense of gratitude for this girl. Everywhere he roamed, life seemed to pass him by except for the bad part of it. The only love he'd known, aside from family love, was for Esther, which had brought him almost unbearable pain.

"You best ride home and forget about me," he said bluntly. "I've taken care of myself in worse circumstances than these. You're taking a chance just riding out here to warn me."

She rose and adjusted her hair. "I had to do it," she said simply and walked to her horse. She mounted in an easy, lithe movement and sat looking down at him. "You will be careful?"

He nodded. "I will. And thanks again."

Anna Belle looked back once and waved as she rode away and then the trees hid her.

Ames had picked up the reins of Cappy and was stepping to the saddle when he heard the sound of a woman's voice raised in a cry of anger—or of fright. It was not quite as loud as a scream but he could hear it distinctly despite the intervening barrier of dense foliage where the descending trail forked. He put the spurs to his horse, and ran him hard through the trees. He had his gun in his hand as Cappy plunged out into the trail.

Two men, dismounted, stood at the head of Anna Belle's horse. They turned startled faces on Ames as he stepped down, holding the sixgun steady on them

80

and advancing toward them with his eyes alight with anger.

"They bothering you, Miss Tate?"

"They—they're Gorton's men," she said, pale and trembling. "I don't know what they meant to do."

"We weren't doin' nothin'," one of the men said. He was a short, stocky cowboy with a bristle of black whiskers on his face. The other one was slim, light-haired and slightly more presentable.

"Stand back from her horse," Ames said, motioning with the gun.

The two men stepped back quickly, both with their arms raised.

"Go on, Miss Tate," Ames said. "I'll take care of these two."

She gave Arizona Ames a swift look and touched spurs to her horse and the animal continued on down the trail. She looked back once before she disappeared and saw that Ames had come close to the two men and was talking to them.

"You fellows unbuckle your gun belts and hang them on my saddle horn," Ames ordered.

"What'll happen if I don't?" the light-haired man asked.

"Drill you clear through and leave you here," Ames said coldly.

The slim man looked at the gun in Ames' hand for an instant, laughed, and said, "She's a pretty girl, so we were just carrying on a bit. We wouldn't have harmed a hair on her head." He began unbuckling his gunbelt. "My maw didn't raise Danny Drake up to be no damn fool target." He walked to Cappy and hung his gunbelt on the saddle horn and stepped back.

He looked at his partner. "Shakey, you better do what he says."

The black-browed man looked sideways at Drake and then shuffled to the horse, unbuckled his gunbelt and hung it with the other.

Ames moved to his horse and mounted, with the same motion sheathing his gun. "Get on your horses," he said. "We're going to town."

The two cowpokes moved slowly to their horses and mounted.

When they were in the saddle Arizona Ames said, "Ride on ahead. Don't go too fast or you'll stop a slug."

When the three-horse cavalcade moved through Shelby it did not go unnoticed. Men and boys walked along behind and the entire group stopped before the jail. The noise brought Sheriff Fraser to the door. He stared in bewilderment for a moment, and then it seemed to dawn on him that something unusual had taken place.

"You can lock up these two," Ames said. He swung about in the saddle and spoke to the man who had identified himself as Danny Drake. "Get down and walk inside. Both of you—inside."

Ames followed the sheriff inside and watched the fat man lock the cell on the two men. Sheriff Fraser moved as though in a daze, for he'd noticed the badge on Ames' chest. After he locked the cell he turned helplessly.

"What's the charge?" he asked.

To Ames' surprise—he had not seen him in the crowd outside—Herman Hammicker slipped in through the door and closed it.

"They were bothering a lady, Anna Belle Tate," Ames said, pleased to have Herman at his side. "I don't know what they would have done if I hadn't come along when I did. The girl's scream brought me at a gallop."

Fraser had recovered his aplomb by now. "That's nothin' to lock a man up for," he blustered.

"You hold 'em until the circuit judge rides through," Arizona Ames said. "Then if the judge says turn them loose, I can't stop you. But not before. Come on, Herman."

The crowd still lingered outside. They looked with curioity and awe at Ames as he and Hammicker made for the hitching rack. Ames got his horse and walked, leading Cappy down the street.

"You can't throw all of them rapscallions in jail," Herman said. "The dad-gummed jail ain't big enough."

"Frazer'll let them out," Ames said. "Gorton won't let them stay there long."

"Then why lock them up?"

"To let them know the law has finally come to Tonto, that's why." Ames grinned and gave the old trapper's shoulder a pat. "For two weeks at least. That's as long as I promised your friend, Kirk, I could stick it out."

"Kirk's not my friend exactly," Herman said. "I mean—I've no right to make that claim. He's too big and important a man."

"So are you, old timer," Ames said. "And don't you forget it."

## XI

In the night, sometime before dawn, Arizona Ames awoke suddenly out of his deep sleep and sat up in the bunk. The Colt hung in its holster near his hand. Herman Hammicker lay fast asleep across the room of the two-man cabin on the Playford ranch. Ames sat motionless, groggy from sleep, and waited.

When the sound was not repeated, he called softly: "Who is it?"

There was a pause, then the door opened quietly and someone stepped inside. Ames got up and struck a match and lighted a lamp. Lanny Ross stood in the doorway. Both he and Ames squinted in the sudden light, in the corner, Herman groaned and squirmed deeper into his blanket.

"What is it?" Ames asked.

"Trouble. The herd we're taking to the Injuns. Seems as how it's not goin' to get there."

Ames began hastily dressing. "Gorton again?"

Ross nodded. "Way I got it figured, the Playford herd is goin' to be substituted by a bunch of scrubs—and some of them with mighty serious cattle disease. Then the good beef goes to Williams for shipping east where the big money is. The Apache get what the little boy shot at. Nothin'!"

"Is Sam going along with this?"

"Sam ain't been his own man for a long, long time, Arizona. You know that better than I do, close as I've been to him. Whatever it is Gorton's got on him sure makes him peaceable."

Ames knew without being told that the crew had spent most of the week gathering some of the prime beef, and the drive had started slowly, so as not to run the weight off the animals. There had been some rumors that seemed well-founded because the herd was held more than a day in one spot, then delayed again, by orders from Playford.

"Last night Sam showed up," Ross went on, as if he knew the thoughts of Ames and himself were at just about the same shared stage. "Told me to drive the herd straight to the railroad at Williams. I asked, 'Well, what about the Apache, Sam? They don't get beef, they'll go warrin' again.' He just looked at me—his eyes don't see nothin' any more—and told me, 'The Apache'll get their beef all right.' Then he told me to ride with him, and he showed me the stuff, and it's a mess. Scrubby beef with not an ounce of fat on it. Just skin and bones. They won't dress out sixty pounds a head if you can believe it! Sam's gone plumb crazy."

"Does Nesta know about this?" Ames asked.

"No, I reckon not. She ain't never bothered much about runnin' the spread, Arizona. Sam's always been a good hand at it—until Gorton got hold of him."

"Did you see any of Gorton's men?"

"They're takin' over the heard when we switch. My boys are goin' to drive them livin' skeletons to the Apache. God help us when the Injuns see what they're gettin'. I'm not much in favor of Injuns, but doin' them dirt like that sure riles me plenty."

"Where is Sam now?"

"He's camped with the boys, way down below the pass. The herd'll be switched some time today."

"All right, Lanny. I'll be along as soon as I can get Herman up."

Ross departed and Ames shook Herman Hammicker, who groaned and swore and rolled over.

"Come on, Herman. Roust out. We're riding."

"Where to?" Herman asked groggily, but Ames had already let the cabin.

The ranch house loomed large and sprawling in the late moon. Ames crossed the porch and rapped softly on the door.

There was a silence, then light shone through a window and a soft voice asked, "Who is it?"

"It's me, Nesta."

"The door's not latched."

He entered and she stood in the doorway holding a lamp. She was wearing a bulky robe and her golden hair was hanging in two thick braids on either side of the pale oval of her face. "What is it, Rich?"

"Where's Sam?"

"He's delivering a herd to the Indian Agency."

"I got word that the herd is to be switched. A bunch of scrub beef is being handed off on the Apache. They'll go hungry this winter if I can't stop it."

"Oh, Sam wouldn't do a thing like that!" she said, her voice rising in shocked protest.

"He wouldn't do it willingly. But Gorton's got something on him. I've got to find out exactly what it is. I've lost too much time already. Do you have any ideas?"

She shook her head. "Poor Sam. I still love him. I guess I don't have to tell you that. I wish there was some way I could help him. But he won't talk to me about it, Rich."

"He must be suffering," said Ames.

She nodded, her eyes suddenly filling. "He's been such a good husband and father all these years, Rich. And then suddenly—" She lifted her head. "It's that Gorton. Oh, Rich, you'd never believe what's true

86

about that man. He's cruel, violent, savage. He doesn't know the meaning of good and I don't think he's capable of any feeling!''

Ames looked at her. "I know he's had his way with Janetta. Has he bothered you, too?'' His face was stern and terrible in its intensity.

She shook her head. "No, not that way, Rich.''

There was a clatter of hooves outside and Herman appeared leading a horse for Ames. He looked at Nesta and said, "Don't worry about Sam. It'll all come out fine.''

She smiled in a way that indicated she didn't think so, and whispered, "I'll pray for you, Rich—and Sam too.''

## XII

Dawn broke magnificently as the two riders emerged through the pass. The herd lay spread out before them, the leaders just straggling to their feet, the vultures circling overhead. A thin splinter of smoke rose from the chuck wagon on the far side of the herd, upwind.

Ames looked at Herman. "Looks like the *good* herd. They haven't made the switch yet.''

Herman looked back at Ames and shoved up his hat. "Reckon today's when they figure to make the swap.'' He spat. "Now I know what Injun-givin' means.''

Ames said, "All right, let's go.''

They came down out of the pass and circled the herd. The cook was calling the hands to breakfast as they rode up and off-saddled. Playford came to meet them, a look of puzzlement on his slightly narrowed eyes.

"Well, Rich, what brings you out here?" he greeted.

"Herman, you go on and get chowed up," Ames said.

Hammicker merely nodded and walked toward the chuck wagon.

"I know what you're planning, Sam," Ames said sharply. "I'm not going to let you do it."

Sam Playford's face went white. He stared hard at Arizona Ames. "You—you wouldn't hurt Nesta, and the boy, Rich?"

"What's that got to do with it?"

Sam Playford shook his massive head. "Oh, God, I can't talk about it, Rich! I swear I can't. It would mean death—or worse for the kid and Nesta!"

Ames nodded. "Seems Gorton has sold you a bill for sure. Listen, Sam, I'm your brother-in-law, a member of the family. You and I were pretty close at one time. You can't shut me out of something as important as this. Now, break loose and let's have it. *Now*!"

Sam Playford wavered. He started to speak and then closed his mouth firmly. "I got nothin' to tell, Rich. Just ride on and forget it."

"I won't ride on, and I won't forget it. What you're doing is crooked and morally wrong as well. I won't stand for it, Sam. You saddle up and ride back to the ranch and take care of your wife and son if you're worried about them. I'll take care of the herd and see it gets to the Indian Agency."

"No," Sam Playford said stubbornly.

"Then I'll have to place you under arrest," Ames said. "It's up to you, Sam."

Playford turned pleading eyes on Ames, from which

88

tears welled. He seemed unaware of them. He said hoarsely, "Rich, God forgive me. Gorton did sell me a bill of goods. He threatened Nesta, and the boy, said he'd maim and kill them if I didn't go along with him. It wasn't an idle threat. He'd have done it, Rich. He's killed a half-dozen men. Shot them down in cold blood. He's the devil himself. I couldn't fight him no more than I could fight a dust devil."

"You take two of your best men and go back to the ranch," Ames said. "Don't leave Nesta and your son out of your sight. I'll take care of everything at this end."

The act of unburdening himself had seemed to strengthen Playford. He nodded, and strode purposefully to the chuck wagon, where the cowboys squatted around eating. "Boys, Arizona Ames here is takin' over this drive," he called out. "Barney and Tadpole, I want you to ride back to the ranch with me." He spoke with decisiveness, and as he swung about and headed for his horse, Lanny Ross looked at Ames and nodded slightly.

Ross slid around until he was standing next to Ames. "I'm sure glad you pulled it off," he said in a low voice. "But Barney and Tadpole are the best guns in the outfit. Are you lookin' for trouble back at the ranch?"

"I never look for it," Ames said, "but sometimes you can't stop it from happening."

"I know what you mean," Lanny said. "I'll go help the boss get saddled up and movin'. Seems there's no time to be lost—if we're goin' to go against Gorton."

After the three riders disappeared, heading for the Playford ranch, Ames called the men together. "There's

89

likely to be gunplay some time today," he told them simply. "If any of you want to go home, now's the time to do it. It won't be held against you. But make up your minds fast."

They looked at him stone-faced.

Lanny Ross chuckled. "You won't find anybody leavin', Arizona. I could have told you that before you spoke out."

"All right, then. When we sight the other herd, start our herd millin' and then herd them into the nearest draw or canyon, or any place where one or two men can hold 'em. There won't be any shooting until I give the word."

Lanny Ross shouted, "Mount up. Head 'em out!"

With low-pitched whoops the cowboys mounted up and began moving the herd out. The bawling cattle created a din as the leaders strung out under the rushes of the fiery little cow ponies. Soon the herd was marching in an orderly compact line due southwest.

Just before noon they raised the dust of the scrub herd. Ames pulled up, took his Winchester from its scabbard and dismounted. Herman reined in beside him. "What you aim to do?"

"It's Gorton," Ames said. "Everybody work the herd into that draw. Then I want everybody back here except two men. You decide which two—Decide among yourselves."

The herd made a slow curve under the urging of the riders. In less than a half hour the last beef disappeared through the brush. A short time later the Playford riders were back, surrounding Ames.

"One more chance. Anybody wants to leave they can—right now."

"Arizona, you sure scandalizin' them boys," Lanny said.

The small herd of bony scrub cattle were standing still now, most of them too sick to move. The Gorton riders were lined up, spread out before the herd and it was now plain that they were onto what was happening.

A rider broke off from the bunch and went at a full gallop off toward Shelby.

"Get him," Ames told Ross and the foreman leaped into the saddle, dug his spurs in, and galloped off in furious pursuit. A burst of fire erupted from the line of riders and bullets zinged through the sage.

Ames put three fast rounds in return, and the riders scattered and there was a yelp of pain. All Gorton's riders dismounted and took cover and began shooting. The Playford men also took cover and set up a steady firing.

Ames crouched and ran through the brush, in a circling movement up a rise. He came to a faint trace of a previous drive and turned into that, moving carefully toward a spot where he would be flanking Gorton. Dashing along in a crouch, the rifle in his left hand and the Colt in his right fist, he nearly stumbled over a man who lay flat on his belly near the top of the hill.

The man had just fired at the Playford men and was shifting his position when he caught sight of Ames out of the corner of his eye. Swiftly, he swung the rifle and Ames triggered the sixgun. Both men fired at the same instant. The .rifle bullet tugged at Ames' hat. Ames took off his hat and looked at the bullet hole in the crown. He looked curiously at the man who had almost shot him. He had never seen him before. He was a broad, chunky, black-bearded man of about forty-five or so. There was a round blue hole between his eyes, which stared sightlessly now.

Ames got the man's rifle and revolver and went out on a point just east of the line of Gorton's men. He emptied every one of the weapons, firing as fast as he could. The Playford men, heartened by the side assault, also began firing and moving forward.

It was too much for Gorton's men. They broke and ran for their horses and those that were able to ride galloped off toward Shelby.

Ames reloaded and holstered the Colt and was packing the empty guns down the hill when he glimpsed a wounded man crawling off into the brush. He dropped the empty guns and bounded after him.

"There's another one over here. Don't know how bad he's hit—so be careful!" he called out warningly. He scrambled down the hill, which was steeper on this side, crossed the trace without slowing and plunged into the brush.

The wounded man rolled over and sat up, holding his hands high. "Don't shoot!" he begged. "I done throwed my gun away."

One of the Playford riders—a man they called Speedy—breasted the brush with wild eyes, and threw a shot at the man on the ground.

"Hold your fire!" Ames shouted. "I want him alive."

Speedy's eyes cleared and he looked at Ames for a moment. "Guess I went crazy for a little bit, Arizona!"

"We all did. Reckon it has to be like that at times.

92

You tell the boys to get the herd moving toward the reservation. I'll be along soon."

He watched Speedy depart in a way that showed how he got his nickname, and then he went to the wounded man and knelt beside him. He'd been shot in the thigh just above the knee, and, except for loss of blood, wasn't hurt badly.

"What's your name?" Ames asked, as he placed a neckerchief around the man's leg and drew it up tight to stop the bleeding.

The man groaned, holding his leg with both hands.

"You're not bad hurt," Ames said sharply. "The bullet hit a muscle and went on through. What's your name?"

"Hedges. Garth Hedges." The wounded man gritted his teeth. "Gawd, I never thought a bullet in the leg could hurt this bad!"

"Was Gorton with you?"

Garth Hedges looked at Ames in amazement. "You must be out of your mind, cowboy!"

Ross rode his horse through the brush nearby and halted. He glanced at Hedges and then looked at Ames. "He got away," he said in disgust. "But I got close enough to recognize him. A man named Dan Drake."

"Maybe it's lucky you didn't catch up," Hedges said.

After one contemptuous look at Hedges, Ross ignored him. He said, "We were lucky, Arizona. Only one of our boys got hit. A flesh wound in the thigh. *They* lost two and this here wounded one."

"He's not hurt bad," Ames said. "He'll be able to ride, all right—and stand trial."

"You're the one who'll stand trial!" Hedges snarled.

93

"Shut up!" Ames rasped. "Lanny, you take over and get the herd to those hungry Indians. Before you leave here I want every one of the sick cattle shot. Then send a good man on to Williams and tell the station agent we won't be needing any cattle cars."

"What're you goin' to do?" Ross asked.

"I'm going to take Hedges to jail," Arizona Ames said, "and then I'm going to call on Slade Gorton."

Hedges began cursing in a strangled voice.

"You've nothing to swear about," Ames said. "Your friends ran away and left you."

## XIII

The man called Dan Drake limped up the stairs to Slade Gorton's office. He tapped on the door and then went inside.

Gorton sat at his desk, with his coat off and his sleeves rolled up. He got to his feet as Drake closed the door, slipped his coat off the back of the chair and put it on. He walked to the window and looked out, then turned.

"Well?" he asked.

Dan Drake had killed men in his time. He'd stolen horses, cows and robbed stage coaches and trains. He'd killed and robbed lonely prospectors and fur trappers. Despite all that he stood in awe of Gorton, if not downright fear.

"Ames drove us off," he said bluntly. "The good herd is at the Indian Agency right now. The scrubs are all dead. That was one little hell of a mess, Mr. Gorton."

Gorton didn't explode the way Drake thought he would. He simply turned and walked to the window and stood there looking out, silent, brooding.

Finally, without turning, he asked: "Why did you leave the crew?"

"Shakey told me to let you know. That damned ramrod, Lanny Ross, chased me until I lost him over toward the creek."

"You're lucky he didn't catch you," Gorton said scathingly. "He's a mean bastard."

"Yeah. Well I had to let you know what happened, or I'd of bushwhacked him."

"Hmmm. Well, here's what I want you to do and don't waste any time about it."

"I ought to let the doc take a look at my leg. I damn near broke it when my horse fell."

"You walked up here," Gorton said. "So don't waste any time with that horse doctor. Gather up all the men you can find. Then get Slink Tate to throw in with you. Take all the men out to Playford's and burn him out. I'm goin' to teach Playford a lesson he'll never forget. Not in the short time he's got to live!"

"What about the women and kids?"

"If they don't get out before the fire starts that's their tough luck. Now get!"

When Drake reached the door, Gorton held up his hand. "Wait!" he said. he was looking down into the street again.

Ames had just ridden into town, and stopped in front of the jail. Garth Hedges sat a horse in front of him. At Ames' command, Hedges got stiffly down from his horse and Ames dismounted and helped him up to the jail door. The two men disappeared inside.

But that wasn't what caught Gorton's eye nearly as much as the stumbling figure of Ted Sullivan coming from the saloon. The boy staggered to a spot directly in front of the jail door and took out a heavy sixgun, eared back the hammer and stood spraddle-legged in the middle of the street, waiting.

Gorton felt a hammering excitement take over. "God damn!" he breathed. "This is made to order, Drake. Is it an easy shot from here to the jail door?"

Drake stood at his elbow. "Easy," he said.

Gorton looked at him with a joyous light in his eyes. "Don't you see? It's made to order! If Sullivan misses, get Ames, then the kid. If Sullivan hits Ames, shoot him down! Get that window open, Drake!"

With the herd in an orderly movement toward the reservation and everything else taken care of Arizona Ames and Hedges rode toward Shelby.

"Ain't goin' to do you no good to lock me up," Hedges said. "Fraser'll turn me loose."

"One of these days," Ames observed, "Fraser'll be locked up himself, for a long, long time."

Hedges laughed. "That'll be the day. Not long as Gorton runs the wagon."

"The wagon's just about broke down," said Ames.

They rode in silence for a long time. Ames had been watching Garth Hedges without appearing to do so. The slim man was handsome, and had a carefree expression, even with the pain of his leg.

"How did you ever get mixed up with Gorton?" Ames asked after they'd rode for a lengthy spell without speaking.

Hedges laughed. "Hell I've known Gorton a long time. We held up a train once, back in Missouri. After he got settled in here he sent for me."

"Why are you telling me you robbed a train?" Ames

asked. "Don't you know that can be used against you in court?"

Hedges laughed heartily. "Hell fire, man. You're not goin' to live long enough to tell any court about me. Gorton'll see to that."

"Long as you feel that way, perhaps you mind telling me what Gorton has on Sam Playford to make him play dog?"

"Big Sam?" A puzzled frown appeared on Hedges face. "You know the kind of people in this world, Ames? The givers an' the takers. Sam's a giver. He's a good man but he ain't got the guts to shoot a man in the back or do another dirt. All Gorton did was tell him what was goin' to happen to Sam's wife and kid if he didn't cooperate. Big Sam thinks more of his family than he does his own life. It's that simple."

Ames had trouble restraining his anger. He was silent because he wanted Hedges to keep talking. The man was clearly touched with fever, and might even be a little delirious.

"Like that time when Sam come in beggin' Gorton to leave him alone," Hedges went on. "Gorton told him, 'Get young Sullivan off Cappy's place and I'll call it quits.' "

Hedges grimaced in sudden pain but went right on talking. "Sam wouldn't do it. All he'd had to do was tell Sullivan to move and he wouldn't. Sam is a big softie."

"Why did he want Sullivan off Cappy's place?"

Ames' horse hearing the familiar name, tossed his head and nickered softly. Ames patted his neck, waitingfor Hedges' answer.

"Gold up there," Hedges mttered. "Old Cappy Turner made a rich strike in that canyon before he

97

died. Gorton wants it.''

"Doesn't Sullivan know about the strike?"

"Hell, no. That boy don't know nothin', Ames."
He lapsed into silence, his face sullen and feverish.
He swayed in the saddle and Ames rode in close to
catch him if he should fall.

They came like that, riding into Shelby, and Ames
got him into the jail only to find Sheriff Fraser gone.
He scouted around and found a set of keys, then un-
locked a cell door and led Hedges inside and helped
him to a bunk.

"I'll get the doctor," he said as he locked the door.

Hedges didn't answer until Ames reached the outer
door. Then he said, "Ames, just to add to your trouble,
I told young Sullivan that you been messin' around
with his wife. I heard he's stayed drunk. Gorton saw
to that. He's lookin' for you, too."

It was with those words ringing in his ears that Ames
opened the door and saw Ted Sullivan standing in the
middle of the street with a cocked gun in his hand.

Ames moved through the door and stood looking
down at Ted Sullivan. The boy's eyes were wild and
his face contorted with passion. "Hard as it is—I've
got to kill you—after what you done!" he called out.

"You can't believe anything Garth Hedges told
you," Ames said in a steady voice. "He's in that jail
right now and soon as a doctor looks at him you can
talk to him and find out he's told you a pack of lies.
He's Gorton's man. Doesn't that mean anything to
you?"

Sullivan shook with the violence of his emotions as
he wavered there in the street. "Make no difference.
I'm going to kill that vicious snake Gorton too—smash
his head. I hate him worse than I hate you. But Hedges

didn't sound as if he was lying—Gorton's man or not. I think it's probably true."

Sullivan suddenly seemed pitiable swaying there in the street. He gripped the gun tighter and yet he couldn't force himself to pull the trigger.

"Ted, it's all part of the play to get your place. Gorton knows old Cappy Tanner found gold up there. He wants to get it. He knows that if I kill you he'll have a free road. Not only to your gold but to your wife!"

Sullivan laughed hysterically. "You kill me? When I've got a cocked and loaded gun pointing right at you?"

"All right, look me in the eye son. If you can't trust me—go ahead and pull the trigger. Only, I warn you Ted, I can draw and shoot faster than you can blink."

Up in Gorton's office, Drake stood at the window, his pistol ready.

"What the hell are they talking about?" Gorton asked hoarsely.

"I don't know," Drake said, almost placidly. "I can't hear what they're sayin'."

"Go ahead, shoot!" Gorton said in an agony of suspense. "Shoot, damn you. Get it over with!"

Sullivan wavered with indecision on his face. His arm straightened and Ames moved with incredible swiftness. His gun roared and at the same moment he saw a flash of motion in Gorton's window and his gun tilted and he fired again.

Drake tumbled through the window and hit the sidewalk with a slack plopping sound. Sullivan stared stupidly at the gun in the dust at his feet and then to his hand dripping red and to the still body of Dan

Drake lying still on the sidewalk.

Sullivan put his hands to his face and turned and ran blindly down the street, ignoring Ames' call for him to stop.

Ames reloaded his sixgun and sheathed it. He looked up at the window and began walking slowly toward the stairway that led to Gorton's office.


## XIV


For the first time in his life Slade Gorton was filled with fear. He hurried down the back stairs as Arizona Ames came tramping up the steps from the main street.

He felt demeaned as he slunk furtively to the barn and quickly saddled a horse. The stableboy came out and stared. Gorton always demanded that this kind of work be done for him.

"Get out of my way!" Gorton snarled and raked the horse with savage spurs. The animal whinnied with pain and stampeded out the open door.

Gorton picked up three of his men straggling back from the fight with Playford. He motioned them into line, and led them toward Slink Tate's ranch.

While the small band of horsemen rode, the man called Shakey told Gorton what had happened. It didn't make Gorton feel any better.

The horses were lathered when the four men rode into Slink Tate's spread. Anna Belle came to the door in answer to Gorton's call.

Suspicion immediately spread across her face. "What do you want?"

Gorton smiled with an effort and removed his hat. "I want to talk to your father," he said in his most civil manner.

"He's real sick," Anna Belle said. "He shouldn't be disturbed right now. He told me not to let anyone in."

"Anna Belle! Who's that?" Slink Tate yelled from somewhere in the house.

"Well, ma'am, he sounds somewhat improved," Gorton said smoothly and dismounted and walked past her and into the house.

He found Tate sitting in the padded chair with a blanket around his shoulders. He wasted no time.

"Ames is on the loose," he said. "We should pitch in, Slink, and put him out of business for good. What he did to you was much worse than what he just did to three of my boys—and to me. And that was plenty bad. He's come close to ruining me."

Anna Belle had followed him into the room. She said, "He's a Ranger, now, Mr. Gorton, with the law behind him."

"You keep out of this, gal!" Tate ordered. "I won't have it, you hear?"

"It was Gorton's men who were bothering me when Rich Ames rode up after me and drove them away."

"Just tell me which ones, and I'll take care of them," Gorton said in his silky voice.

"Now, did you hear what Mr. Gorton said? Go on to your room. I'd hate to take a stick to a gal that's a grown woman. Now git!" The old man spoke with such fierceness that Anna Belle quailed.

Without another word she left the room.

Slink Tate looked at Gorton with distate. "He's got you on the run, has he? You don't need answer me—I can see he has. You wouldn't be here if it weren't so. Tell me, Gorton, how's it feel to have Arizona Ames breathin' down your neck?" The old man tittered.

Gorton controlled himself with an effort. "He won't be breathing for long," he snapped. "Well, how about it, old man? You're sitting there not able to move by yourself because of an Ames bullet. Don't you want to even the score?"

"I'd give my soul in hell to put a bullet in his belly. In his heart, too."

"Then let me use your men. I can do it for you. And I'll come back here and tell you how it happened. Right down to the last kick."

"Yore a pretty good talker," the old man said in a soft voice. "That tale ought to pleasure me some. All right, Gorton. I don't know where the hell they are. But round 'em up and tell 'em I said they're to take orders from you."

"I need fresh horses."

"The corral's filled with fresh horses. Take your pick."

"All right." Gorton whirled, and almost ran from the house.

Arizona Ames came into the stable just minutes behind Slade Gorton. The stableboy saw him coming and turned to run. But Ames grabbed hold of him and swung him around.

"Where did he go?"

"Mr. Ames, I don't know for sure but I think he headed out to Slink Tate's place!"

"Saddle a horse for me."

The stableboy moved with commendable speed, saddling up a rangy gelding. He leaped back into a box stall as Ames mounted and drove the animal through the big double doors.

Ames rode the animal until the lather poured from its flanks, without spurs or whip. It seemed to sense that the utmost was needed, and responded without lashings, eating up the miles to Tate's place.

When Ames came riding into the ranch yard the three men who had accompanied Gorton were just starting to cross to the corral, Gorton having gone on ahead of them in his fierce impatience to pick a fast horse for himself. Ames had his sixgun on the startled riders even before they recognized him.

"Don't reach and you won't die," he shouted warningly.

Slade Gorton was about sixty feet further on, close to the corral, and when he looked back to see what was delaying his men he saw them standing docilely with their hands raised high.

The trait that made Slate Gorton a dangerous man was not in his skill with a gun but his utter disregard for human life other than his own. He slipped the big revolver from a holster under his arm and steadied it against a broken wooden drinking trough that had been dragged outside the corral fence, so that it could either be carted away or chopped up for firewood.

Gorton cocked the piece with a thumb made slippery from sweat and sighted down the barrel. He felt absolutely no emotion other than complete concentration on sighting in on his target. His finger contracted slowly. He squeezed the trigger and as the hammer went down the gun roared and buckled in his clasp.

He saw Arizona Ames fall as though his legs had been knocked from under him. In almost the same instant he saw a bloom of smoke from the falling man. Slade Gorton stumbled back and dropped his gun, feeling the hot tearing of lead in his chest. He tried

103

to keep from falling and found he couldn't. His shoulders hit the ground. He attempted to rise and discovered he could not move. Darkness came down slowly. It did not lift.

Gorton's bullet had struck Ames in the right thigh, inches above the knee. It was a superficial wound, the bullet having passed clear through the fleshy part of his thigh. And though the heavy-caliber bullet had knocked him off his feet, he managed from his prone position to keep his gun trained on the three men who stood there frozen, with startled expressions on their faces.

"Take off your gunbelts and let them fall," Ames directed.

It took them barely an instant to realize that the man on the ground wasn't out of action. The three gunbelts plopped to the ground.

"Now get on your horses and ride. Take Gorton with you. If you're still in town when I get back I'll lock you up or kill you." He motioned with the pistol as he struggled to his knees and then to his feet. "Move!"

He kept them under his gun while they carried Gorton's body to his horse and draped it across his saddle. The four horses, with three riders and a dead man, started toward town.

Ames felt a wave of dizziness pass through him, shaking him. His leg numb at first began to ache. He staggered and would have fallen except that Anna Belle Tate, appearing suddenly after the riders left, held him upright. He leaned heavily on her as she guided him toward the house.

The move up the steps into the house and up the

stairs took the last of Ames' strength. He collapsed onto a bed in Anna Belle's bedroom with a low moan. Anna Belle undressed him, cutting his right trouser leg off while old Slink Tate ranted and raved from the ground floor below.

"Get that killin' bastard out of my house!" he kept screaming, over and over again.

The wound was swollen and angry looking, but Anna Belle appeared with basin and towels, and went right to work on it.

She spoke once: "Does it hurt?"

"It's beginning to," he said. When she poured alcohol into the wound he bit his lip until it bled. Then Arizona Ames passed out.

## XV

Arizona Ames woke up, not instantly alert, trying to tell Anna Belle that he was sorry to have passed out. His eyes came into focus and he could see it was dark and that Anna Belle hovered above him. A yellow lamplight glow made the room golden.

She smiled shyly, leaning over him. "You've had a good sleep," she said. "It helped you very much." She placed a cool hand on his forehead.

"What time is it?"

"Nearly eight. Are you hungry?"

"I—I believe I am."

"That's a good sign," she said and left the room. Ames put the covers down and looked at his bandaged leg. It was on a pillow. His clothing hung on the back of a chair. He tried to sit up and then slumped back, his face twisted with pain. From the door, Anna Belle pushed a huge tray through, saying, "Don't try to get up."

She placed the tray on the table beside the bed and began tucking a cloth under Ames' chin. She sat on the edge of the bed and deftly began to spoon a thick soup into his mouth.

"I believe I can do that," he said.

"Later. Right now let me do it. You lost quite a bit of blood and I imagine you're very weak."

"I should get back to Playford's," he said weakly between bites.

"For goodness sake why? Everything is fine over there."

"Well, I should see young Sullivan—"

"He and Janetta came by yesterday, asking about you."

"Yesterday? Why it was late—what day is this?"

"You've been here three days now."

"Oh, Lord, I can't believe it!"

Ames raised his head, listening. "I don't hear your father."

Anna Belle smiled a gentle smile. "Oh, he hasn't shouted for all of two days now. He's come to accept having an Ames in the house."

"Who convinced him?"

"Everybody, I suppose. Sam Playford come calling the first day, waving a white flag. He said the country's growing up and the people ought to do that too. Then Captain Will Kirk came by and gave him a talking-to. By that time he began to be pleased that he's playing host to the most famous man in Arizona."

"Good Lord," Ames groaned. "I've got to see Kirk and hand in my Ranger shield. I still can't ever see myself as a Ranger."

"We're all very proud of you," Anna Belle said contentedly.

"Well, I hope they feel as good about me next week as they do now."

"Don't worry, they will." She wiped his lips with the cloth she took from his neck. "Your mother brought a letter from Colorado. Do you want to read it now?"

"I'd be obliged," he said.

Anna Belle took the tray away and returned shortly with the letter which she gave him. She watched him as he opened the envelope and removed the sheet of paper.

It was from Halstead.

*Dear Arizona Ames*

*We all miss you up here on the Troublesome. Fred is married and the boys said to tell you hello. I just want to remind you that you're half-owner of this spread and if you're not going to claim it maybe you'd rather have the money. Let me know.*

*Best regards, yrs. resp.*

*Halstead*

"Not bad news, I hope," Anna Belle said.

Ames eyes were closed. He said, "No, not bad at all. Colorado rancher just reminding me that I'm half-owner of a spread up there and asking me if I'm coming back."

She stopped all movement, her hands poised before her. Suddenly she straightened and stared hard at him. "Are—are you going back?"

"I don't know."

"You're not a boy. Can't you make up your mind?" Her voice was almost sharp.

He grinned at her. "It all depends on a girl I know."

"A girl?" She turned slightly pale.

"Yes. A girl with big purple eyes who knows how

107

to feed a man lying flat on his back—''

"You don't know what you're saying! You can't mean—''

"Just give me time to get back on my feet."

Anna Belle fled to the door and stopped there. She turned and stared at him again, giving him an impish look.

"You'll have your chance," she said. "Just try and escape!"

Ames glanced through the window at the night outside and saw the bright, unblinking light of a million stars. He thought of Esther without pain, for the first time. He sighed and said, "Just so I get that chance. That's all I ask."

A succession of people from the Tonto Basin came through the room in the days that followed.

Captain Will Kirk came calling with the amnesty papers. He laid them on the bed. "You earned these, Rich Ames. There are no conditions attached. I'm sorry you refused to keep that badge but I understand how you feel about being as free and independent as the four winds. There are some men you can't ever pin a lifetime badge on, even though you'd give a great deal to be able to. Remember, you can come back any time you want to, Ames. We need men like you."

His mother, Sam Playford and Nesta, and young Rich, the Sullivans, Herman Hammicker accompanied by the twins Mescal and Manzanita, all paraded through his room, loving him, wishing him well and wanting him back among them.

Now and then he heard Anna Belle and Slink Tate shouting at one another but gradually Slink's shouts grew weaker and weaker and the day came when a couple of Tate cowhands brought the old man into the room.

He looked at Ames with his gloomy eyes and said sharply to the two cowboys, "Take me a mite closer. My eyes ain't what they used to be."

The cowhands brought the old man to the edge of the bed. Slink Tate put out his hand. "Things have changed," he said. "You're the new breed, Ames. Welcome back to the Tonto Basin."

Arizona Ames looked over old Tate's shoulder and saw Anna Belle peering down at him and there was no mistaking the message in her eyes. He took Tate's aged, slightly tremulous hand and pressed it warmly. "And you're the new breed now, too," he said. "Maybe more than I could ever be. It makes me proud to be the friend of a forgiving man."

"I won't deceive you, son," Tate said. "It wasn't easy."

"I know," Ames said, nodding. "It took more than ordinary courage to blot out all the long years of pain and invalidism from your mind, to tell me that you've given up everything that hating me has meant to you. It was something to cling to and now it's gone. Thanks for having that much courage."

Tate looked away out of the broad reach of the Tonto Basin, as if he didn't want Arizona Ames to see the moisture that had collected in the corners of his eyes.

# THE RAID
# AT
# THREE RAPIDS

# I

Midnight. No moon, but if there had been one, it would have been hidden behind a blanket of scudding clouds. The basin which lay in the desert below Gila Mountains was pitch-black, as though a shroud had been laid across the farm and ranch land. The mountains rose against the steel-blue sky, etched in back ink. A coyote howled; suddenly stopped.

Midnight. Ike Weaver suddenly found himself strangely awake, mind alert, ears attuned to the soft whisperings of the wind his body bathed in a cold sweat. He lay still for a moment, with the instinctive caution of one who has lived all his life in the west.

He checked the rough-hewn bedroom of the house with his eyes. A shaft of light from the bedded fireplace in the other room played shadows on the ceiling, on the lodgepole pine that made up the walls.

Weaver swung his gaze to the opposite wall and saw his three brothers soundly asleep in their bunks, the rhythmically rising and falling of the quilts calming him momentarily.

Then he heard a noise, a faint, metallic click as though a gun had been cocked or a boot had hit a stone. Or was it his imagination? Was there movement in the shadows, someone inside the small ranch-house?

A wood stump in the hearth suddenly emitted sharp, crackling noises as the coals hit some pitch, and there was an explosion of fire and sparks. Yes! There *was* someone there! The silhouette of the person was clearly visible in that split second against the wall.

Weaver jumped from the bed. "Pete! Doug! Henry!" he yelled. He grabbed for his old Sharps rifle which he kept by his bed. "Raiders!" He charged for the next room, cursing.

A flurry of movement across the boards of the house, and then the loud report of a rifle and the dense white cloud of smoke, and Ike Weaver screamed. He crumpled to the floor, a bullet through his hip. His brothers tumbled from their bunks, dressed as they were in nothing but long shirts, scattering as they did so, clutching their rifles as they dropped to the floor. There was another shot fired from the living room, and then the raider appeared briefly at the doorway.

The three brothers and the wounded Ike Weaver knew what they were going to see even before the raider showed himself; knew it from the constant rumors and talk which had been at the tongue-tips of every rancher and nester in Gila Basin for the past few months.

They knew—but it didn't help any. They were frozen into wide-eyed, horror-filled statues. None of them were particularly superstitious, would have laughed if they had been strangers to the area. But there was no denying their eyes, not when all four saw the same thing.

There, framed in the doorway, was a hideous, grinning specter. A glowing skeleton, topped by a death's head with fire-brand sockets for eyes, its fleshless mouth ripped back in a wild, demoniacally fiendish grin.

And from the depth of whatever hell had spawned the ghost rose a hollow, chilling laugh which curdled the marrow of the four Weaver boys.

As quickly as the apparition had appeared, it disappeared in sudden blackness, its macabre laughter floating on the wind behind it. There was a clinking of a metal can, the faint sloshing of liquid, and before any of the men could gather the courage to act, the whole front room burst into light, licking flames.

"It's—it's real!" Doug Weaver gasped. "By God, and it's burning us out, just like the others!"

Smoke billowed into the bedroom, choking them. Ike, still sunk to the floor and gripping his torn hip to stop the blood, cried out weakly, "Get me out of here! Don't leave me to them!"

"We won't, Ike!" Henry said. He crossed to his brother and put his arms around the wounded man's chest. "C'mon, fellahs, help me. We got to move fast before the fire gets us all!"

Doug and Pete ran over and helped lift Ike Weaver up, then the four of them staggered from the bedroom, into the only way out, through the now raging inferno.

They coughed, choking, and their eyes watered and stung until they were half-blinded; but they ran for the door and stumbled into the front yard. A volley of bullets sent them scurrying and groping for cover behind their buckboard, which was drawn under the cottonwood growing off to the left.

The farmyard around them was like a scene from some vivid nightmare—though the four Weaver brothers knew that what they saw was all-too-terrible reality. The wraith-like figures of the ghostly

115

nightriders—and their skeletal, glowing horses—rode wildly about the blackened grounds, screaming banshee sounds that shattered the night into broken fragments.

Some held burning torches in their bony hands, and even as the Weavers watched, helpless, pinned down by the sporadic fire of other raiders, the barn and the livestock pens and the small lean-to which had been built for the horses were set afire. Flames leapt high into the black sky, destroying in a matter of minutes what it had taken the four recently-settled brothers months of arduous labor to build as they attempted a profitable farming of the potentially fertile lands of the Gila Basin.

When the fiendish killers had completed their grisly task, they banded together at the entrance lane to the Weaver farm, still shouting and screaming, still sending volleys of shots at the hiding place of the Weavers and preventing the boys from returning the fire except intermittently and without aim. Then, as one, they spurred their horses along the lane, their spectral bodies glowing dancing light in the darkness.

The four Weavers came out from their concealment and stood up in a slump-shouldered, dejected group, watching the retreating forms. All the buildings around them were blazing infernos of flame and black smoke now—the dream of four young, hardworking, honest men dying in fanning, searing heat. There was no chance to save anything of their belongings, or of their livestock or horses, they knew as they watched the flickering figures grow smaller and smaller in the distance.

"Damn 'em!" Henry Weaver shouted suddenly.

"Damn 'em, damn 'em!" There were tears of frustration and rage brimming in his eyes.

"They finished us off, just like they done plenty of others in Gila Basin the past few weeks," Doug Weaver said. "They've burned us out complete."

"And they ain't ghosts, either," Ike Weaver said, trying to staunch the flow of blood from his wounded hip. "Ain't no ghosts fire live ammunition. You mark my words: it's real live men behind this here raiding and killing around Three Rapids, and whatever it be, there's some lowdown reason behind it, too!"

And in the far distance, at the head of the fleeing band of marauders, the leader chuckled coldly to himself as he spurred his horse onward, looking back over his shoulder at the orange glow rising high into the night sky from the burning farm dwellings.

It wouldn't be long now, he thought to himself; it wouldn't be long at all before all the small nesters in the Gila Basin were either burned out or running like scared rabbits from the awesome fear the ghost-like killers had instilled with their night raids.

He spurred his horse on still faster, leading the others back to Superstition Cemetery, whence they had come.

## II

Arizona Ames felt the blast of fire-hot air as he swung off the steps of the train. It was mid-June in Prescott, but already the oppressive heat of Summer baked the bustling territorial capital.

Ames walked to the large overhang of the depot, and in its shade, he removed his sombrero and wiped his forehead with his sleeve. Then he fitted the hat

117

carefully back on, picked up his carpetbag, and facing the late afternoon sun, he began to stride down the dusty main street.

Prescott, Arizona, had an Indian heritage, the white man having rarely explored north of Gila until American domination, and consequently many of the buildings were flat-roofed adobes, with a row of butt ends of cottonwood logs protruding about a foot at the place where an *anglo* house would have eaves.

This made the stately, near Victorian looking Grand Union Hotel where Ames was heading a unique and readily identifiable landmark. The Grand Union was the best Prescott had to offer, and the newest, for it had been built after Arizona had become a territory and Prescott needed a place worthy of visiting dignitaries and politicians. Normally Ames would not have stayed in such a grand and fancy hotel, but this was a special occasion, a very special one indeed.

The fight for recognition as a territory had been a long and frustrating one for Arizona, dating all the way back to 1856, when a delegation had gone to Washington, D.C. Until 1863, the Congress had ignored the request, many Northern members fearing that the party in power in Arizona was pro-slavery. But in December of that year, an itinerant government had set out from the nation's capital, having gained recognition, and Prescott was chosen as the territorial capital.

That had been a few years previous, but still the citizens of Arizona were filled with a highly contagious public spirit, and patriotism for their territory still filled the air of Prescott, filled it as surely as the veneer of heat.

Ames and his neighbors were imbued with an almost

118

aggressive nationalism, and they fought and worked to build a future State. Many a Texan took a back seat to an Arizonan when it came to bragging about one's home.

It had been this deep love for Arizona which had spurred Ames across half the territory and to Prescott. It had been this—and the dead-of-night summons from its governor, The Honorable David Lee Cardwell.

The thought of the wax sealed letter which had been handed to him by a nameless, never-speaking rider two days earlier made the tall lean cowboy finger reflectively his shirt pocket where the note lay folded. He didn't take it out and read it again; he didn't have to. He had memorized its few terse lines the first time

*Mr. Rich Ames: Would appreciate your presence in the private lounge of the Hotel Grand Union, Prescott, evening of June 17th, ten o'clock. Wear regular clothing and secrecy is vital. Matter of utmost importance, concerning the welfare of the territory.*

It was signed with the distinctive, Old-World caligraphy of Governor Cardwell.

Ames had been at his brother-in-law's, Sam Playford's, ranch in Tonto Basin. From the standpoint of the ranch, it was an inopportune moment to leave it, for there was much to do with the advent of the long, dry Summer months. Yet Ames did not hesitate but sent the messenger back with the word that he would be there. He didn't have to know the reason; it was sufficient that he had been asked. His nickname after all, was Arizona.

Ames slapped dust from his pants and shirt on the

steps of the Grand Union, and then walked into the lobby. Its ceilings were high and chandeliers hung from them, casting yellow glow. The floor was carpeted and the reception desk was of massive oak with a marble top; the staircase was broad and ornately carved; and the dining room specialized in French cuisine.

The Grand Union was one of the first monuments to gracious living in a land of roughness, wildness, and at times, savagery.

The desk clerk caught the steadfast glint in Ames' eyes and knew that this man was more than a saddle-tramp or outlander. There was purpose and bearing inherent in this large, well-built man, in spite of his less than well-groomed attire. "Sir?"

"A room," the Arizonan said. "The name is Ames."

"Sir!" The clerk was suddenly all action. He rang the silver bell on the desk and a porter appeared. "Sir, a room has already been reserved. We have been expecting you. If you will sign, the boy will show you to your room. And may your stay be pleasant."

Ames printed his name in the register, then followed the boy, who actually was a stooped, wizened old man, as he carried the carpet bag up the stairs and down the hall of the second floor. The lower the floor, the greater the prestige, for climbing many flights was more than some of the older statesmen could handle.

The room, if not the finest, was one of them, and a steaming hot bath was already drawn in the porcelain tub which was in a draped-off alcove of the bedroom. He had been expected, all right.

Ames undressed and washed, and when he was finished the water was gray and gritty from the accumulation of dust the open windows of the train had deposited on him. Then he lay down on the canopied bed, for he had time for a three hour nap before his meeting.

At eight o'clock he rose and dressed in clean but similar clothing as he had arrived in, and descended to the dining room. He was sitting back after a fine meal, enjoying a cigar and thinking about finding out from a waiter where the private lounge was, when the man who had delivered the governor's message walked up to him.

The man was now wearing a black-and-white check cheviot suit and a string-tie, and his black boots were to an almost patent shine. He bowed slightly, his face still as bland and as average as to defy remembrance. "Mr. Ames?" he said, "We have met before. My name is Smith."

Ames smiled up at the man, remembering how he had looked when he had ridden up to the ranch, bone-weary and filthy dirty. "Yes, Mr. Smith. Good to see you again."

"Follow me, please."

Ames walked with Mr. Smith through two large parlors filled with impeccably dressed men and women, and then down a narrow hall. At the end of the hall, Mr. Smith stopped and swept aside a scarlet curtain which was across a doorway.

He motioned for Ames to enter, which the cowboy did, and then the curtain dropped and Ames was alone in the small room.

The lights were low and the windows heavily draped, and it took a moment for Arizona Ames to adjust his eyes. Then he saw that he wasn't alone, but that there was a man sitting at an ornate round table toward the back. The man was facing him, a stylishly dressed older person with long silver hair and a luxuriant beard. The man stood and beckoned to Ames.

"Take a chair, please. It is a pleasure to meet you at last, Mr. Ames. Your name is, well, to put it bluntly, something of a legend in the West."

Ames came nearer, and was struck by the man's rich, full voice, and for a moment thought of him as a Shakesperean actor. Then the man said, extending his hand, and standing, "Permit me. I am Governor Cardwell."

"The pleasure is mine," Ames said, shaking his hand.

It took a lot of man to impress Ames, and Ames was impressed. He liked Governor Cardwell right from the start, liked his manner, his firm grip, the way he looked the Arizonan straight in the eyes.

Ames could tell that beneath the frock coat and ruffle shirt was a rockhard quality which had done much to mold Arizona, and would continue to for as long as possible.

They sat, and the Governor produced a cut crystal decanter and two snifters from the sideboard. "Perhaps a small drink, Mr. Ames? A fine brandy, if domestic. The new vineyards in Northern California . . ."

Ames nodded. The brandy was warm and flavorful, and he savored what for him was a rare treat. The Governor said, "I'm sorry, but I don't have much time, Mr. Ames. The work is pressing, and nobody knows I'm here except you and Mr. Smith."

"I have kept my end a secret as well," Ames said. "My sister and her husband are the only ones who know I've come to Prescott, and even they don't know of this meeting."

"Good, good. Captain Kirk said you were a man of his word."

Captain Will Kirk—the mention of his name flooded Ames' mind with the picture of the stern, brown-faced Arizona Ranger. It had been Kirk who had made Ames a temporary Ranger when he had returned to Tonto Basin after years of being a renegade, and to many an outlaw and killer. It had been Kirk who had given Ames the amnesty signed by the very man who now sat across from him.

"I had heard of you a long time before Captain Kirk talked to me, and quite frankly, I can tell you I had my doubts. But after the magnificent way you handled the trouble there at your home, I can see he was right about you. He was always sorry you refused to wear the badge permanently, but he respected your need to be free.

"When I asked him to recommend one of his own men for this mission, he said to contact you first, that your lone resourcefulness and love of your land made you the best man available. And, by God, I believe him."

Ames, a modest man after his years of hardship and wandering, grew uneasy from the praise from so prominent a personage. He shifted in his chair.

"I live as I believe, sir," he murmured.

"Consider that as of this moment you are my special agent, Mr. Ames. A special—and may I add—secret—emissary responsible to no one except myself."

Ames, for all his experience and worldliness, was overwhelmed by this high honor.

"Thank you, sir," he said simply, yet with deep, heartfelt feeling.

"You may not thank me when you hear why I sent for you," the Governor said.

He reached inside his coat and produced a map of the Southwest. He spread the heavy paper out on the table and moved the milk-glass lamp closer. He placed his finger on a small dot near the Mexican border, nearly on the Gila River.

"Three Rapids," he said. "An insignificant flyspeck among many such towns of the Gila Mountains. At one time this whole area was booming with gold placer mines, but since 1869 it has become almost deserted, the giant share of our mining now coming from the lodes around Tombstone."

"Isn't that where the new Sangre River dam is being built?" Ames asked.

"Yes. The town of Three Rapids is on that river, and is the location of the dam site, which is to begin erection immediately. The Sangre River is the largest one feeding the Gila, and when the dam is completed it will turn the whole Gila basin from the arid wasteland it is now into a fertile belt for ranches and farms.

"The dam will provide irrigation and flood control the whole year round, and it will be a prestigious and economic milestone for the Territory. It will certainly help us gain our Statehood."

"I still don't see—"

"You will, Mr. Ames. There's been trouble down there, trouble of a peculiar kind. From the reports I've been getting, we seem to be fighting the ghost of Three Rapids' cemetery!"

"Ghosts?" Ames said incredulously. "There aren't such things as ghosts."

"Impossible or not, there is a reign of terror in

Three Rapids which, if unchecked, will stop the dam from being built.''

Ames frowned and leaned on the table.

"Tell me about these ghosts," he said.

"In a small valley slightly west of Three Rapids is a large burial ground first used by the Indians and later by the miners from all over the surrounding country. Superstition has it that the ground is sacred and must be left undisturbed.''

"A common belief among Indians and the uneducated," Ames said.

"Yes, and most of the locals are just that, uneducated. The smart ones left after the gold dried up and are either in the Gila basin below the town or where mining has proven profitable. But even so, it still doesn't account for the appearance of mysterious, spectral riders on skeleton horses coming out of the graveyard and burning and ravaging surrounding homes and the dam site, and I'm afraid, even killing.''

"Is there any pattern or reason for these attacks?''

"Not in the usual sense, no. But the locals swear it is because of the dam, for when it is completed, its back-up waters will inundate the cemetery.'' The Governor began to fold the map. "Now understand, Mr. Ames. I don't believe in ghosts any more than you do. When I heard of this, I sent two top investigators to Three Rapids. One was shot dead.

"The other said that he followed the ghosts or spirits or whatever they are back to the cemetery, and there they just vanished. He said nothing could drag him back there, and I'm afraid his opinion is voiced by most of the workers at the dam. They are threatening to leave, and if they go, the dam is finished before it's started.''

Ames sat back in his chair, stunned. The dam was one of the most important projects to the Territory. It was sorely needed by the farmers and ranchers of Gila Basin, and needed by Arizonans as a whole as a bid for Statehood.

If the dam failed because of midnight, ghostly raiders, it would turn Arizona into the laughing stock of the United States, and the Congress would think the Southwest was peopled with silly, ignorant children, unfit to rule themselves. Failure of the dam was worse than having no dam begun! And yet—it sounded impossible.

"I don't believe it," he said, shaking his head. "I won't believe it until I see these ghosts myself, and I know very well I never will. There has to be a mundane reason for it all."

"You're going to get that chance, Mr. Ames," the Governor said flatly. "The main construction of Sangre Dam is to start once a hundred and fifty thousand dollars is received at the bank in Three Rapids for workers' pay and supplies. There is a special train leaving tomorrow afternoon, going straight through to the dam site with that money on board.

"It will be guarded of course, and along with the money there will be delegates from all parts of the Territory, representing their area interests and seeing what they can learn and use for their own use. You are going to be on that train as a delegate from Tonto Basin. Actually, you will be representing me.

"I want you to find out what's going on there and put a stop to it. There won't be much time, for the construction will commence immediately and the delegates will be returning. If they return with stories of

126

ghosts riding through the night, we will be in serious trouble."

"I understand," Ames said grimly. "I'll do my best."

"I'm sure of that," the Governor replied. Suddenly he looked up, over Ames' shoulder, and when Ames turned he saw Smith standing in the doorway.

"I must leave now," Governor Cardwell said, rising from his chair. "All messages will go through Mr. Smith here, care of this hotel. I'm sure you understand that if I was directly involved publicly, it would only add credence and authenticity to an already untenable situation."

Ames stood up, shaking the Governor's hand again. "Yes, sir." To make sure, he asked, "You said that the train leaves tomorrow, afternoon?"

"Correct. Smith has your ticket." The Governor walked to the door, then turned and said, "Oh yes, the other delegates are either here in the hotel now or will be arriving tomorrow. You will be meeting them at breakfast or lunch, I'm sure."

He smiled, though it was a weary and saddened expression. "Good luck and Godspeed, Mr. Ames."

### III

The train from Prescott bound for Three Rapids hurtled through the hot, muggy Arizona night, and the monotonous sound of the wheels singing over the steel rails lulled Ames into a drowsy state. It was past ten now, and he had just come to the coach from the smoker, where he and the other area delegates had cigars and brandy following a full meal.

By nature a taciturn man, Ames had joined in the

127

evening's conversation only minimally. He had found most of the other representatives to be politicians of one type or another—a lawyer from Phoenix, a councilman from Tempe, a large landowner from Flagstaff—and while they were all pleasant, dedicated men, Ames did not have a great deal in common with them save where his homeland was concerned.

He was a solitary individual, one who, for fourteen troubled years had been a renegade, a drifter, a legendary figure with an awesome reputation for a lightning draw equaled by but a scant few throughout the West. He was a product of the range, at home nowhere as much as under the winking stars, a nomad without roots, living day to day and never really finding true peace and happiness.

Ames had set to the trail when he was merely a lad known as Rich Ames in Tonto Basin. There, he had revenged the seduction of his beautiful twin sister Nesta, killing the man responsible as well as the town's crooked sheriff. It was fourteen long, arduous years later before Ames returned to his birthplace, answering an urgent summons for help from Nesta, and was able to clear his name.

During the brief stint as an Arizona Ranger which Governor Cardwell had spoke of, he had saved Nesta and her husband, Sam Playford, from the evil and power-hungry Slade Gorton. And, too, he had briefly fallen in love with Anna Belle Tate, the daughter of one of the men who had been in that gunfight in Tonto Basin those many years past, and whom Ames had maimed with a well-placed bullet from his .44.

Wanderlust was still strong in Ames' blood then, and so he soon grew restless and eager to move on. That was why he had left the Rangers, and Anna Belle, and had once again ridden the dusty trails of the West, a man alone.

He had traveled to the Dakotas, and immediately had become involved with a crooked gambler named Jersey Jack Kelson. Framed for a murder he had had nothing to do with, Ames had nearly lost his life in a blazing ghost town high in the Gold Buttes, attempting to save the lives of the widow and the son of one of the men Kelson had killed behind the guise of his traveling Dollar Wagon. But justice had triumphed, and the Arizonan had captured the gambler and cleared himself with the sheriff of the town of Phileaux River, and thus had been allowed to move on.

The episode had taught Arizona Ames a wise lesson, though. After a short period of more aimless drifting, he had known where his destiny lay at long last and he had returned to Tonto Basin. He had come home for good. He had gone into partnership with Sam Playford to maintain and further build his brother-in-law's holdings. The Arizonan put himself into the task with passion and fervor; the love affair he had hoped to renew with Anna Belle Tate had not come to pass, for she had married another man soon after he had left that second time.

Ames' new life in Tonto Basin was a good one and a quiet one, except for a few short weeks when he had gone to Gallows Valley, in Northern Nevada, to negotiate the purchase of several thousand head of prime beef for the Playford Ranch from land baron Wade Lamont.

There, he had found himself in the middle of a near-range war, managing at the last moment to avert a bloody carnage and save the lives of Lamont and a beautiful young nester girl named Jan. But for the first time in his long and turmoiled life, he had found the roots he sought, roots whose seeds had long ago been sewn in the time of his childhood.

Arizona Ames was, at long last, a contented man.

At that moment, however, in the train coach bound for Three Rapids, he was also a mighty uncomfortable man. He disliked long train rides to begin with, preferring the open rangeland and the familiar saddle of his faithful sorrel Cappy, and what with the trip from Tonto Basin to Prescott, and now this ride to Three Rapids, he decided ruefully that if he didn't see the inside of a train car for the rest of his life, he would not regret it a moment.

The heat did nothing to appease his discomfort; even though all the windows were still opened wide, and the train was moving at a considerable speed, the air both inside and out was thick and choked with dry acridity.

He would not sleep much this night, he knew; the stifling Pullman car was not the most ideal place to get a rest. And there was his mission in Three Rapids. The Governor's solemn, urgent plea for Ames to bring a quick end to the trouble there still echoed in his mind, and he knew the matter of the Sangre River Dam and the so-called ghosts threatening its erection was no small one.

Still outwardly drowsy, though his mind was alertly working now, Ames stared out through the window at the rushing Arizona countryside. He wondered what could bebehind the ghostly raids on the Gila Basin area. There were simply no such things as ghosts, and nothing short of a spirit shaking his hand in broad daylight with the sun shining through it was going to alter his belief.

Obviously, that meant live men were behind the raids, the terrorism, which abounded around Three Rapids these days. But why? Maybe it had something to do with the Sangre River Dam project; there was still an element in Arizona which opposed statehood for one reason or another. Could that have something to do with it?

Ames shook his head slightly. It was still too early for speculation. He would have to wait until he had arrived in Three Rapids, talked to those citizens who had seen the "ghosts" first-hand and had an opportunity to do some investigating on his own, before he formed any sort of opinion. Besides, Governor Cardwell would want substantiated facts, not uncorroborated guesswork.

As he sat there, pondering, Ames was suddenly aware of eyes on him and he swiveled his head away from the open window. Across the aisle, facing him, was a tall flaxen-haired girl in her mid-twenties, wearing a tailor-made blue summer suit with bell sleeves.

She was trim and very cool-looking, and her lightly-tinted red mouth was pursed. She studied Ames frankly with large, dove-gray eyes that were the dominant feature in a smooth, milky-complexioned and very beautiful face.

The Arizonan shifted uncomfortably under her steady gaze, and smiled sleepily back at her. Boldly, then, the girl got to her feet and came over to where he sat and seated herself directly across from him. She said in a soft, clear voice, "You're Arizona Ames, aren't you?"

"Yes, ma'am," he replied, surprised.

"Are you with the delegation to the Sangre River Dam?"

Ames hesitated. Then he said, "Yes'm, I am." He wondered who she was.

As if sensing his thoughts, she said, "My name is Priscilla Franklin, Mr. Ames. I live in Three Rapids—or more properly, in the Gila Basin below it. My father is Will Franklin. I imagine you've heard of him."

Ames had. Mr. Smith had briefed him, after his talk with Governor Cardwell yesterday, on the influential citizens in and about Three Rapids. Will Franklin's name had been prominent on the list. He was perhaps the largest landowner in Gila Basin, and was the most outspoken opponent of the Sangre River dam.

It was his contention that its construction would allow the nester families in the area to grow bigger, thereby injuring his large and prosperous holdings and those of the other established ranchers. He was an opinionated man, Smith had said, and an obstinate one. A man who had fought doggedly for every inch of ground he possessed and who meant to keep it; any way he could, as he'd stated publicly on more than one occasion.

Ames said non-committally, "Yes, I've heard of your father, Miss Franklin."

"Priscilla," the girl said. "And may I call you Arizona?"

"I'd be pleased."

She nodded. "I've been in Prescott visiting relatives. My father wanted me away from Three Rapids because of all the trouble in the area of late. You know about the ghosts, of course."

"I've heard of them," Ames said laconically.

"What do you think?"

"Ma'am?"

132

"You don't believe in ghosts, do you?"

"No," Ames said. "I don't."

"Well, neither do I," Priscilla said firmly. There was something which might have been fear and pain in her eyes now, and bitterness was in her voice when she continued. "I think the raids and the killings are the work of real men, hired killers and the like. And I—I think my father is involved with them."

Ames was unprepared for that. He sat up very straight on the coach seat, frowning. "What makes you say that?"

"The way he's been acting lately. He's been against the dam project right from the beginning, and he was almost unbearable for awhile with his opposition. But then these raids started, and he's cheered up considerably. It's almost as if he's happy that people are being burned out of their homes, killed—"

The Arizonan said, "And that's why you think he's behind the terrorism?"

"Not exactly behind it, but certainly involved," Priscilla said. "I think he and some of the other large ranchers banded together, and hired these—these murderers to play at being ghosts."

"Do you have any definite proof of this, Miss Franklin?"

"No," she said, "only my suspicions. I probably shouldn't be confiding in you like this, Arizona, but you have such an unimpeachable reputation that I thought you could—well, talk to my father and get him to stop these terrible pillagings."

Ames was about to reply that if Will Franklin was indeed responsible for the ghost raids, he would have to stand trial under the law; but before he could say the words, something caught his eyes from outside the

133

rushing train. He turned his head, staring through the window intently, and in that moment he saw in the distance some dozen separate, eerily-wavering glows bunched closely together. They were approaching the train at a rapid clip, flickering spectrally in the dark black moonless night.

Priscilla turned her head to follow his gaze, and her mouth opened wide and a gasp escaped her throat. "What—" she began.

Ames got quickly and unceremoniously to his feet, his right hand slipping down to rest on the .44 nestled in the black carved holster ornamented with a large silver "A" on his hip. He began to make his way swiftly along the car toward the door at the upper end, watching through the windows the phantomlike scintillas approaching the train.

He had just gotten his hand on the door latch when there was a sudden screaming rend of metal on metal as the train's mechanical brakes were applied. The car shuddered violently, and couplings thundered together as the rolling stock bean to slow, the wheels still shrieking on the steel rails in protest.

Ames was thrown hard into the door. He bounced off it, reeling backward, and crashed into one of the coach seats. From the other end of the car, Priscilla Franklin cried out in fright and two of the delegates who had been in the rear began to shout painfully and confusedly as they were flung from their seats.

Ames regained his balance, jerked open the door, and gained the platform outside. The .44 was in his hand now. The train had slowed almost to a standstill, and the Arizonan ran to the metal steps at the side of the platform. The ghostly shapes were almost upon the train now, and Ames could see the skeleton-like

134

features and outlines of both horses and riders, gleaming bones and leering, hideous skulls.

But the barrage of gunfire which suddenly came from the spirit riders, peppering the train mercilessly, ricocheting lead off the metal plating of the car and the platform railing, was very real. Ames threw himself flat on the platform, squeezing off several answering shots with his .44.

Several of the silvery figures jumped off their glowing mounts and, under cover of the fire from their cohorts, ran toward the baggage car at the front of the train, three cars from where Ames was.

The money, the Arizonan thought immediately—they're after the money. But there was nothing he could do. He was pinned down where he was, unable to move. He hoped the governor's territorial guards would be able to stop them. They were heavily armed, and there were four of them entrenched inside the baggage car with the hundred and fifty thousand dollars.

Sporadic gunfire reverberated throughout the blackness of the night. The ghost killers had taken their mounts into the pinon juniper and greasewood which lined the raised mound of the railroad tracks at that point, and were firing from in there. Their eerie luminosity made them appear to be like flitting fireflies in the protective growth.

Then, all at once, there was a tremendous, echoing explosion, and the night sky lit up brightly from the direction of the baggage car. Ames felt the solid, jarring impact where he lay, and he knew immediately that dynamite had been used to blow open the car. He began to curse softly but vehemently, feeling helpless with the bullets singing and whining over and around him.

There was more rapid gunfire from the baggage car, and then all was quiet from there momentarily. But another explosion seared the night finally, a much smaller one this time. Minutes later, the Arizonan had a glimpse of four or five spectral figures rushing into the juniper and greasewood. Then the shooting stopped altogether.

Hoofbeats replaced the pistol and rifle fire, retreating rapidly, and Ames could see the ghost killers hightailing it away from the train at full gallop, the flickering phosphorescence growing smaller until once again there was only a bunched series of dancing glows fading on the horizon.

Ames jumped down from the platform and ran to the baggage car. Some of the other passengers and delegates, as well as the engineer and part of the crew, came rushing up as he did. There was a gaping, blackened hole in the side of the car. Apparently, one or more sticks of dynamite had been flung through one of the specially fitted gunports in the wall of the car.

Inside, the four territorial guards lay amongst the smoking rubble. All of them were dead; those who had not been killed by the dynamite had been shot to death in cold blood by the spectral raiders.

The door to the large safe at one end of the car had been blown off as well. The safe was empty.

The hundred and fifty thousand dollars earmarked for the beginning of construction of the Sangre River Dam was gone.

## IV

The train arrived in Three Rapids nearly three hours late, and minus the baggage car. When finally the train shuddered to a halt alongside the plank wood platform and shed which served as the station, it was ten and the sun overhead was hotter, if possible, than in Prescott.

Arizona Ams swung down, then he turned and helped Priscilla Franklin off the hot iron steps. Around hi the other delegates were descending and milling around the platform.

Some were cursing, some were mopping their brows. All were still shaken by the night's ordeal.

Priscilla's face had a pallor, and terror still etched lines around her pretty mouth nd eyes.

The confusion on the platform was great. There had been a party of a half dozen townspeople waiting for the train since early morning, and they rushed forward, obviously concerned over its delay, and then the delegates began to talk and gesture, relating the tale of the raid. The noise and hubbub made Ames think of a calf-branding roundup, and he stood back from the crowd with the young woman next to him.

Most of the delegates as well as the train personnel were congregated around an overweight, swarthy man with a coppercolored face more wrinkled and battered than the Big Four Stetson he wore. His cartridge belt and holster were low on his Levis, and occasionally the sun glinted off the five-pointed star pinned on his cotton plaid shirt.

The old sheriff listened patiently to the encircling mob, a somewhat bored look on his face.

Ames knew it would be pointless to talk to him at the moment, so he picked up both his and the girl's carpetbags and began walking toward the shed, Priscilla following without a word.

Suddenly a hoarse shout called over the crowd. "Pris! Pris, there you are!"

The girl spun around in the direction of the cry, as did Ames. A young man came running towards them, shouldering his way through the throng. He looked to Ames to be about twenty-three or four, a tall if slightly thin individual dressed like a farmer: dungarees, lightweight shirt, brightly colored neckerchief, and a belly nutria Montana hat set on an angle. A few locks of shiny black hair tumbled over his forehead and he brushed them aside as he took off his hat and approached Priscilla.

Priscilla blossomed into a warm smile, color coming back to her pale cheeks.

"Gene!" she cried out, "Oh, Gene!"

And impulsively she threw her arms around the waist of the young man. It was obvious to Ames that this man was her beau, and she, in turn, was definitely his girl.

"It was so terrible," she said in a choked voice. "The ghost-garbed riders—" She was unable to continue. She buried her face in his shirt, and began to cry.

"Pris, honey . . ." Gene soothed, folding his arms protectively around her. "What happened? What's this about ghosts?"

Ames was about to introduce himself and explain, when another man suddenly appeared out of the crowd, a man whose anger was evident in his ruddy complexion and balled fists. He was big—big in girth, height, stance. He was somewhere in his early fifties, and wore grey worsted pants and a round-cut sac style black summer coat. His high starched collar looked as though it was chafing him, and his derby seemed too tight and out of place.

He was, Ames judged, one of the local leaders, and who had dressed especially for the occasion, though would be far more comfortable in work clothes.

"Unhand her, Cameron," the older man snapped. "Let loose of my daughter at once, or so help me I'll make one less nester in these parts myself!"

Gene Cameron sprang from Priscilla, startled.

"I'm sorry, Franklin," he said, though his tone was one of coolness rather than contriteness.

Priscilla Franklin turned to her father, anger flashing in her eyes, where seconds before they had watered with tears. "One less nester, you said. That's all you think about, hurting people. Isn't four dead guards enough killing for one night?"

"Now hold on, daughter," Franklin said.

"I won't!" Priscilla lashed out, stamping her foot. "Not any longer. You've thrown your weight around, forcing the farmers out of the Basin, trying to stop the dam any way you can, hating Gene here just because he's poor and struggling to make something of the land! And now—now the train has been robbed and Sangre River dam may never be built. I hope you're proud of yourself!"

"You act as though I was behind it," Franklin said, shocked at his daughter's sudden attack. "I never knew about—"

"Don't tell me that. What kind of father are you?" With that, she spun and dashed down the length of the platform, sobbing into her hands.

Cameron gave one quick glare at Franklin and then ran after Priscilla, calling her by name. Franklin watched his daughter and Cameron, anger making his lips thin white lines. Ames studied him, wondering if the man had really been unaware of the raid until this morning, or whether his actions were nothing more than a smoke-screen.

After a long moment, Franklin turned to Ames, glowering. "You, stranger, what's your name?" he demanded.

"Ames," the Arizonan said simply.

"You were on that train, Ames. What was she talking about?"

Ames related the events, concluding with, "We had to clear the boulders from the tracks which had been placed there as an obstruction. Then we discovered that the baggage car was too damaged to roll, so we uncoupled it and tipped it off the tracks." Franklin shook his head. "Those infernal ghosts."

Ames eyed him squarely and said slowly, "You believe in them?"

"I don't know what to believe any more," Franklin said. He looked up at Ames. "But what's that got to do with you? Who are you to stick your nose in private affairs?"

"I'm one of the delegates, Mr. Franklin. The Sangre River Dam is very much my business; is everybody's business in the Arizona Territory."

"A delegate, eh?" Franklin jabbed a finger at Ames. "Well, I said I'd meet you fellows this morning, but that doesn't mean I'm going to talk to you. I think that dam is a mistake, a costly mistake, and that's all I'm going to say about it." He looked down the platform at where Priscilla and Cameron were talking.

He clenched his fists again, and without another word to Ames, started toward them.

Ames felt sorry for the daughter and Cameron; bucking a man as obstinate and powerful as Franklin invited disaster. Yet, in this case it was a private affair and one in which Ames could be of no help.

Ames saw that the sheriff had dispersed the delegates, and that the train crew were walking away, leaving only two other men with the lawman, both of them locals. Ames took one more glance at Franklin and Cameron, who were now yelling at one another, then walked over to the sheriff.

The sheriff looked up as the bronzed Arizonan approached and shaded his eyes with his hand. "Yep?" he asked around a plug of tobacco.

"I'm one of the delegates. The name is Ames, and—"

"Not *the Ames*," the sheriff cut in.

"The one sometimes called Arizona," came the reply.

"Figures," the sheriff said. "Heard of you down in Mongollon about ten years ago when you came through. When all those old geezers were squawkin' to me earlier, your name kept popping up. Ames did this, Ames did that. I thought it might be the same man."

"Pleased to meet you, Mr. Ames," the man on his right declared, suddenly sticking his hand out. "My name is Celtas, Neal P. Celtas of the Southeastern Cattleman's Exchange and Trust Bank. Mighty glad you're here."

Ames shook the banker's hand. Celtas was small,

barely five feet high, yet he was dressed almost to the point of pomposity. He was in a double-breasted Prince Albert coat and striped pants and wore a highly fashionable black square crown hat. He looped his thumbs in the pockets of his coat.

"It's high time a little gumption came to Three Rapids," he said. "My bank stands to lose a great deal because of the robbery last night."

"Neal," the sheriff said in studied patience, "Neal, that money didn't belong to the bank. You were only going to store it here a spell, that's all."

"Abe McGivern, you old fool," the banker said to the sheriff, "my bank holds mortgages on the nesters in the Basin. Without the dam, there won't be the water they need to grow crops and raise stock. Sure as sunrise, there will be foreclosures, which is exactly what the bank doesn't need. We need interest off the loans and fat, prosperous customers, not a bunch of worthless land."

Celtas faced Ames. "It's more than that, Mr. Ames," he said. "I was branch manager here during the boom days, though when the town dried up, I was forced to go back to the headquarters in Gila Bend. I'm president, now, but Three Rapids is like my home to me, and I wanted personally to re-open the bank here and see the community grow again. Call it sentimentality, if you will."

Sheriff McGivern deigned comment, but spat out a thin stream of brown juice, narrowly missing the banker's boots. This seemed to infuriate Celtas.

"I've been after Abe McGivern here to do something, Mr. Ames," he said with fury. "He's too mule-headed to worry about it. And now this! This train robbery!"

142

"Nothing I can do," the sheriff replied calmly.

"What about gathering a posse and trailing the robbers?" Ames suggested.

"Don't need to track 'em. I know where the trail leads."

"Where?"

"Same place they always go. To the cemetery. I've been out there a good half dozen times since the trouble started, and that's where the trail always ends."

The man on Ames' left began to chuckle.

"Don't see nothing funny," the sheriff said. "If I were you, Cass Bryce, and had made as large a bet as you did with Will Franklin, I'd be cryin' about now."

"Sure I bet him that the dam would be built on time," Cass Bryce answered smugly. "But I bet a lot of the nesters that it wouldn't be finished at even better odds. Hell, I even have a little pool going as to the day and hour it's completed."

Bryce laughed again. "In case you'd care to wager about the dam, Mr. Ames, or anything else, I'm usually at the Golden Pick."

"I'll remember you," Ames said.

He appraised the gambler, marking him as a cardshark and oily little vulture. He was dressed in tinhorn garb of cutaway frock coat, string tie, brocaded vest, and black vici kid shoes. His face was angular and gaunt, like one of the skeletal visions Ames had seen the night before, and the thin horizontal mustache only heightened the effect. He was smoking a slim cheroot, and by the looks of the soiled shirt and ash spots on his pants and coat, he smoked a cigar most of the time.

Ames turned back to Sheriff McGivern.

"Reckon I'll join the other delegates at the hotel," he said.

143

As tempted as he was to ask the sheriff more questions about the supernatural events in Three Rapids, he knew that too much curiosity, especially in front of Cass Bryce and Celtas, the banker, might endanger the secrecy of his mission. He nodded to the other two men, shaking Celtas' hand once more, and then started down the main street of Three Rapids.

On his right was the long, straight stretch of now empty track. The train had immediately pulled out of the station and headed toward the deserted roundhouse and still usable water tank about a mile further along. On his left, Ames passed the town's buildings, only some of which had reopened since Three Rapids' revival.

There was the Golden Pick saloon facing the station platform; the sheriff's office with its galvanized tin roof, which Ames was sure would turn the office into an oven; the mercantile store with a freshly painted sign over its open door; the funeral parlor doing land-office business as of late; and the biggest single dwelling, the Crystal Palace, which was now boarded up with sagging roof, tangles of brush and debris piled against its walls and against the curb of its sidewalk.

There were more decaying structures, and then Arizona Ames reached the hotel, which was little more than a sprawling, one-story house. He climbed the stairs and stopped to scratch a sleeping dog behind its ears, and then he opened the front door and went in.

After checking and depositing his bag, Ames left, heading for the telegraph office, which was just to the other side of the bank. He carefully worded a telegram to Smith at the Grand Union, outlining the raid, and then he walked to the livery stable.

# V

Three Rapids' livery stable was a sod-roofed building at the near-end of town. A weathered, canted sign over the double entrance doors stated that the proprietor was one Lucian Hevis, and that iron forging was a specialty. Arizona Ames pushed open one of the doors and stepped into the cool, familiar-odored interior.

Lucian Hevis turned out to be a lean, lanky man with a bald pate and a salt-and-pepper, carefully waxed handlebar mustache. He had frightened rodent's eyes and an uneasy manner.

"Help you, mister?" he asked Ames.

"I'll need a good saddle horse for a couple of days," Ames told him. "I'm with the territorial delegation to the Sangre River Dam project."

Hevis moistened his lips nervously, his eyes flickering everywhere but never meeting Ames' steady gaze. "Reckon I kin let you have one, all right. Gelding set by you?"

"That'll be fine."

"You want him rigged out?"

Ames nodded.

"Be four bits a day, plus feed," Hevis said. "Set by you?"

Again, the Arizonan nodded. Hevis grunted, turned and moved to one of the stalls in the back, where a sleek well-curried gelding stood quietly. He took a three-quarter rigged saddle from a stack of similar ones on the wall nearby and began to outfit the animal.

When he was finished, he brought the gelding over to where Ames waited. The Arizonan gave him a half-dollar, rubbed the gelding's muzzle lightly, easily, and took the reins from the livery proprietor.

"Can you tell me how to get to the Three Rapids Cemetery from here?" Ames asked.

Hevis' entire body jerked convulsively, and his sallow face went an unhealthy gray color. His rodent's eyes were terrified. "You—you ain't fixin' to ride out there, are you, mister?"

"It was on my mind," Ames told him laconically.

"Listen, mister, mebbe you ain't heard 'bout Superstition Cemetery. They's things go on out there that ain't natural."

"You mean the ghosts, is that it?"

"And worse," Hevis said tremulously. "Nobody goes out to Superstition Cemetery, nobody in their right mind, mister. The miners and the Injuns what's buried there don't cotton to live folk prowlin' among 'em. I'm tellin' you, mister, you go out there, chances are you'll end up dead. Dead as them what's in that graveyard."

"Suppose you let me worry about that," Ames said. Hevis' fear was a tangible entity in the coolness of the livery stable, and the Arizonan had never felt easy in the presence of cowardice.

"Now how do I find the cemetery?" he asked again.

In a trembling voice, Hevis told him. Then he turned abruptly and scuttled off toward the rear of the stable, as if Ames was already a dead man whose presence there was an ill omen.

The Arizonan let the gelding outside, mounted him, and rode south out of town, as per the livery proprietor's instructions. A half-mile beyond the limits, a dusty, little-used trail wound off to the west. This would eventually take him to the small valley which housed the Three Rapids graveyard, Supersitition Cemetery.

146

Ames rode slowly in the late afternoon heat, finding that the gelding was a good, capable animal, though no match in stride or carriage for his sorrel Cappy. As he rode, he thought back to what Priscilla Franklin had told him just before the attack on the train the night before—and upon what had happened in Three Rapids today with Will Franklin and Gene Cameron. Was the girl right that her father was behind the killings, and now the robbery of the Sangre River Dam money?

Franklin has impressed Ames as a blustery, stubborn, egotistical man. But a party to murder and pillage? It was possible, of course, especially with the bet he had made with the gambler, Cass Bryce. Or perhaps Bryce was somehow involved, possibly as a front man for other interests. Ames had him pegged as an unscrupulous type who would stop at nothing to gain his ends. There were a lot of possibilities, the Arizonan thought, but no definite probabilities just yet.

Ames reached the small valley just past four. The blazing sun was a white-hot globe suspended in the brilliant cobalt blue of the Arizona sky. The valley was small and narrow, grown with mesquite and greasewood and a few cottonwoods and cedars and the giant saguaro cactus indigenous to the area.

The cemetery lay in the center of the valley. It was several hundred yards square, protected on three sides by cottonwood and cedar thickets. The trees cast thick shade over parts of the graveyard, and gave the false impression from a distance of a cool oasis.

The first thing which struck Ames' eye as he neared the burial ground was the huge stone crypt which sat at its far rim. It was stark and gray, of neo-Grecian design, with a sloped roof and three huge, ornate Cor-

147

inthian pillars fronting it. The bleak coldness of the structure seemed to cast a pall of foreboding, of malevolence, over the entire graveyard.

Arizona Ames felt a brief chill touch his shoulder blades as he dismounted at the rusted iron gates which bordered the entrance to the cemetery. He looped the gelding's reins around one of the upright bars on the near gate and walked through.

Immediately he noticed the interlocking and overlapping hoofprints of perhaps a dozen horses which covered the grassy earth. They seemed to have come in together through the gates through which he had just passed, and then to have branched out in various directions. The same was true in reverse, the prints coming together just inside the gates as if the horses and their riders had joined just before riding out again.

The prints seemed to end, on those branch-outs, at various grave sites.

It was as if the horses and riders both had come out of the mounds of earth, and later had returned there when their nights of murder and carnage were completed.

Ames set his teeth grimly and moved further into the cemetery. It was very quiet now; not even the call of birds or insects could be heard. All that would be needed, he thought ruefully, was a whistling wind and the appearance of wraithlike figures floating on the stifling summer air.

Moving slowly, his eyes carefully canvassing the area left and right of him as he moved, Ames threaded his way through the headstones and plain crosses and completely unmarked mounds which dotted the rough ground. Most of the markers were small and unadorned, though some here and there were ornately

148

carved of heavy granite, denoting the final resting places of well-to-do miners who had died both natural and violent deaths during the placer boom of several years earlier. These were emblazoned with such epitaphs as:

*Here lies Samuel Parker, Kilt Dead In The Golden Pick Saloon Over An Ace Of Clubs;* and *RIP Hoss Donnel, Who Died In Bed At The Crystap Palace;* and *Easy Ike—A Right Generous Man With A Nugget.*

Ames made his way to the huge crypt at the far end of the cemetery. Up close, the structure was even colder, more unearthly than he had first imagined it to be. He stepped up to the heavy iron door, sealed as if it had been when the remains of the man who had had it built were put inside. On the wall next to it was a huge bronze plaque which read:

JEDEDIAH HARRISON
1816 - 1868
THE RICHEST MAN
IN THESE HERE PARTS

There was a bas-relief figure of a man with a pick and a nugget pan below the inscription, and then the words: *No Man Deserves A Better Resting Place.*

Ames smiled wanly at the obvious self-esteem in which Jedediah Harrison had held himself. Then he walked slowly around the squarish crypt, his gaze searching the area for some sign of the ghost killers, some clue as to what had happened to them after they had ridden in there. He absolutely refused to accept

149

the fact that they really *were* ghosts, and as such had returned to their graves to rest until the next nocturnal raid. Logic, which the superstitious citizenry thereabouts failed to use, told him that even if the ghosts of the miners and Indians were able to rise from their burial places, where would they get *live* horses upon which to make their forays into the surrounding countryside? Skeleton horses didn't leave hoofprints.

But the Arizonan found nothing. He prowled amongst the graves, careful not to trod upon any of them—out of respect for the dead, rather than from any fear of supernatural reprisal. There was no sign of any living humans having been in the area at all recently, save for the hoofprints which were plainly evident. There was an answer in there somewhere, he knew that. The question was, *where*? If he could only find some clue.

The report of a carbine shattered the late afternoon stillness, and a bullet seemed to come out of nowhere to send Ames' sombrero spinning from his head.

The Arizonan had faced rifles and pistols, both directly and from ambush, on innumerable occasions during his long and oft times violent life. His reactions were honed to their sharpest edge. He flung himself prone in one smooth movement, turning his body slightly to the left so that he would take the impact of the ground on his left shoulder. At the same time, his right hand was pulling the .44 from its holster on his right hip, finger curling around the trigger.

He rolled once, across a patch of thick grass, and came up propped on his elbows behind one of the large granite headstones, the .44 at ready, just as the carbine cracked a second time from some unseen sniper's

150

point. Chips of granite flew off the edge of the head-stone, showering down on Ames' back.

He put his head around the marker cautiously, trying to locate the source of the fire. He saw nothing. The air was completely still now, charged with a static electricity. Ames felt sweat flowing freely on his body as he lay listening and waiting behind the epitaph.

Ghosts didn't have Winchester or Springfield carbines that fired live ammunition, he thought. It was a walking, breathing, two-legged polecat behind that rifle. But where had he come from? And were there more than one? Ames had been over every inch of Superstition Cemetery in the past hour, and he had seen and heard nothing; and with everything as still as it had been, he would surely have heard any approaching rider.

Well, wherever the ambusher was situated, his purpose was clear. He didn't want Ames, or anybody else, prowling around the graveyard. That would tend to indicate that something was to be found there, all right, something the Arizonan had overlooked or failed to recognize.

He had no idea what it could be.

He lay in the silent heat, his body tensed, for perhaps ten minutes more. There were no more shots, no sounds of movement or activity at all. Had the sniper gone? Ames decided that he couldn't stay where he was indefinitely. There was one way to find out.

Carefully, he raised himself into a crouch, still hidden behind the headstone, and then he levered up and ran in a low, crab-like stride across a section of open ground to where a big-boled cedar grew. The rifle cracked again as he gained the tree's cover, hammering bark off the trunk. The ambusher was still out there.

But he wasn't shooting to kill, Ames thought. He had waited until the Arizonan was behind the cedar before he had fired. A warning—then, get out, or else. The shooter would remain wherever he was entrenched until Ames left the cemetery. If he didn't, there would be a slug with his name on it before long.

Ames nodded to himself. All right, then. He would leave, just as he was supposed to. But he vowed grimly that he would be back. And when that time came, he wouldn't allow himself to be chased away.

He quit the protection of the cedar and worked his way through the thicket toward the entrance to the cemetery. He wasn't fired upon. But when he left cover to once again move across open ground toward the gates, the carbine sounded from its unseen location in the graveyard and a slug went screaming high over Ames' head.

The Arizonan ran full speed, not looking back, pretending fearful flight. He reached the gelding, unwound the reins from the gate bar, and swung up into the saddle. Turning the animal abruptly, he put spurs to its flanks and rode away from there at a full gallop.

When he had left the small valley, he slowed the gelding to a canter. Anger had flushed his cheeks and made his temples pound. He did not cotton to being shot at from ambush. He was now more determined than ever to get to the bottom of the mystery surrounding Superstition Cemetery.

Even if the welfare of the territory of Arizona, and the people of Gila Basin, had not been concerned, even if he had not been made a special agent to Governor Cardwell, he would have been just as determined. It had now become a personal fight now.

## VI

The sun was waning as Arizona Ames returned to Three Rapids, striking the lean and now angry Arizonan in the back. He left his gelding at the stable, instructing that the animal be fed and rubbed down, and then he walked to the hotel.

The lobby was more like a parlor, with a worn Oriental rug on the floor, a large red-based kerosene lantern suspended by gold chains from the low ceiling, french doors on his right leading to the dining room, worn wooded stairs opposite, and a chewed-up wooden counter on his left.

Ames reached across the counter and took his room key from one of the pigeon holes, for there wasn't any clerk present, and after washing he came back downstairs and went into the dining room.

The dining room was also the town's only restaurant, so it didn't surprise Ames to see some of the locals eating at the scattering of tables as well as the delegates. On one side of the french doors sat the sheriff and the banker, both ith steaming bowls of stew before them. McGivern was chewing his food methodically, but Celtas was busily talking and waving his knife for emphasis. The sheriff didn't seem to be taking much, if any, notice to the stream of words.

McGivern looked up as Ames entered. "Evenin'," he said. he indicate an empty chair next to him. "Join us?"

"Mighty kind," Ames replied and sat down. "Evenin', sheriff, Mr. Celtas."

"Good to see you again, Ames," Celtas said. "I was just telling Abe here that—"

Again he was cut off by the sheriff. McGivern asked, "Locate the cemetery all right, Ames?"

Ames smiled thinly, not answering.

"Just happened to be passing some time with Hevis, and he dropped the fact you were headin' that way," the sheriff added, and returned to his eating.

"You were there?" Celtas asked, leaning forward. "Excellent! What did you find?"

"Nothing much," Ames said with a shrug. He suddenly doubted that the sheriff just happened to have been gossiping with the hostler, or that the first impression of him being slow and dim-witted was correct.

A plump, cheerful Mexican woman came to the table, rubbing her chubby hands on a bright red apron. She, Ames knew, was also the desk clerk, maid, cook, and owner. Had been, she'd told him when he'd registered since her husband had died some years ago in a mining accident.

"*Buenos tardes,*" she said with a wide smile.

"Have the *estafado,*" McGivern suggested. "It's the specialty of the house, bein' the only food she cooks usually."

"Looks good," Ames commented, and then said to the *señora,* "*Estafado, por favor, y café negro.*"

"*Si,*" she said, and then in broken English she continued, "*Señor* Ames, a message for you." She reached into the pocket of her apron and produced a folded slip of paper. She handed it to Ames. "*Un joven hombre* said to give this to you. He came in the afternoon, looking for you."

"*Gracias, señora,*" Ames replied.

The note was from Gene Cameron, and in carefully blocked letters the nester had written: *Must talk to you*

154

*about the raiders. Come to my ranch anytime tonight.
I'll be waiting for you.*

Ames folded the note and put it away. He was puzzled by Cameron now. Was the nester somehow aware of his mission here? If not, why had Cameron gone to him and not the sheriff? Or was this some kind of trick? Was Cameron part of these raiders and Priscilla Franklin suspected the wrong man? Had Cameron sent the note in the first place? The *señora* only identified the message bearer as a young man.

There was only one way to find out. Ames said to the sheriff, "How do I find the Cameron spread?"

"It's in the basin, bottom of the mountains," McGivern answered. "Just follow the main road out of town. When you get to the Ebner place, take the left fork. Couple of miles and you'll see a gate and a sign. That's Cameron's."

"The Ebner place, then left fork," Ames repeated.

"You'll know the Ebner place on account of the house," the sheriff added. "Old man Ebner got tired of building after he put up the sides, so the roof is ten-ounce duck." He eyed Ames through half-lidded eyes. "Going out there tonight?"

"Might," Ames replied: "But at least not until after dinner."

Celtas left shortly after that, and as the sheriff proved almost as taciturn an individual as Ames, the conversation which had been lively, if one-sided, with the banker's presence, dwindled to near silence. Ames left the hotel after finishing a second cup of coffee and rolling a smoke, and returned to the livery stable. Then he rode out of Three Forks in the opposite direction to the cemetery.

Once the road down the mountain side had been

155

used a great deal, but now it was in sad repair. The dam laborers would all have arrived by train, and the farmers of the basin had closer and easier stores to frequent, making the trip to Three Rapids one done by solitary and infrequent riders.

The road was long and arduous; steep, twisting and treacherous. The gelding walked, at times feeling its way, for much of the underfooting was soft and loose, with sudden dips and holes. Dry, brittle grass and nettles and small cacti rose in odd clusters and tufts among the chinks and crevices, and the dust was thick and heavy.

The autumnal colors of the boulders and cliffs were still discernible in the twilight—reds, burnt umbers, bronzes, yellows, muted with the growing shadows. Around him in the distance, Arizona Ames saw the jagged, blunt spires of the buttes, their outline against the deep blue sky like giant black molars.

Eventually the slopes gentled, though the area lost little of its savage, sterile appearance. The dusk lengthened into indigo, deep purple, and gray as the sun dropped beyond the horizon, and still Ames rode in a slow jog. Then he saw a thin plume of smoke ahead, and as he neared it, he made out the peculiar outline of the Ebner house.

It was unique, even here in a country of oddities. The box-like house of wood walls rose barely above a man's head in height, and then was capped by what looked to Ames as a weatherbeaten and frayed wedge tent. A chimney flue was on the other side; from it the wisp Ames had first noticed. Just beyond the trail branched four ways. The Arizonan rode the left fork, as instructed.

He headed north, skirting the rim of a large crater

156

whose bottom was lost in inky darkness. Much of the land was deeply eroded and filled with the debris of flash floods, and once more the Arizonan was reminded just how important Sangre River Dam would be to the Territory. From the Gila to the border, the parched earth had little surface water, artesian wells being used instead, yet after the Summer rains, thick grass grew and the cottonwoods of the washes and the cedars of the mesas filled out, testifying to the fact that the earth was not barren, only extremely dry.

Near a large growth of mesquite, Ames noticed a rough-hewn gate set between stone cairns, and on the gate was a sign painted with Cameon's name in the same careful lettering. Ames dismounted and opened the gate, then urged the gelding down the narrow wagon path, which was little more than two ruts side-by-side.

He passed over a rise, and then saw the bleak, silent ranch of the nester. Nothing moved, not a sound disturbed the night air; the house lay darkly shadowed under the new moon, only a pale glow from one of the windows telling Ames it was inhabited.

Ames approached, passing the empty corral and the tall, narrow barn which was on his right. The house itself was new, but already the weather had taken its toll of the wood and adobe. As he dismounted the door flew open and Cameron spotlighted by the interior light behind him, stood framed in the doorway, pistol leveled.

"Who's there?" the young nester called out.

"Ames."

"Ames?" Cameron said, and holstered his weapon. "Good. C'mon in, and share a cup of coffee with me."

157

The coffee was bad, tasting of bitter boot leather, Ames thought as he sipped the hot brew moments later. It wasn't surprising; Cameron, like many impoverished cowboys, boiled and reboiled the beans until there was nothing left except the husks.

Ames sat at the home-made table in a square-backed chair and studied the spartan room, bare of everything except a stone fireplace and hearth, working gear, and absolute living essentials. There was another room off to one side, but it was hidden by a blanket stretched across the doorway.

Cameron stalked up and down the small room, hands clasped behind him, forehead furrowed with a frown. "I wanted to see you earlier today, Mr. Ames, but you had gone someplace. I left you a note. Thank you for coming."

"Call me Arizona," Ames said. "But I don't understand why you wanted me. There's the sheriff—"

The nester snorted. "That old buzzard. He's older than these hills, and besides, he's a friend of Will Franklin." He shook his head. "No, Priscilla said she had confided in you on the train, and I'll have to agree with her. You're about our last hope."

"Miss Franklin is as pretty a filly as I've seen," Ames said. "You're a mighty lucky man."

Cameron blushed. "If'n it weren't for her father," he said and then paused. He walked over to the coffee pot and poured himself a cup in a tin mug. "He'd like nothing better than to run me off my land. Me, and every other nester in the basin."

"Why?"

"He used to have this whole territory, Arizona. He didn't own it, only used it, before the days of fences and neighbors. He was the only cattleman for a

158

hundred miles in either direction almost, and he wants those days back again.

"He's been fighting us ever since we started moving in, and the Sangre Dam is his last battle. When it's finished, so is his dream of an empire. That's why he's behind all these lootings and killings. That's—"

"Wait," Ames said. "Miss Franklin thinks her father might be involved somehow. Are you telling me you think he' actually the leader of these raiders?"

"I'm not thinking it," Cameron said hotly. "I know it." He sat down across from Ames. "My land is adjacent to Franklin's, Arizona, and every time there's a raid in the basin, the riders cross my land into his. True, the best way to the cemetery is that route, but that doesn't explain one thing."

"What's that?"

"Why these ghosts disappear when they cross over onto his property!" Cameron leaned forward intently. "This story about them being the dead miners and Indians is of course pure nonsense, cooked up by Franklin to scare the locals. I've followed those riders as they've returned, even followed them last night, and damned if I can see how they do it.

"They're visible, flickering and dancing with that glow of theirs, right up to a gully near one of Franklin's line shacks. They never get out of that gully that I can see, yet when I get there, they've vanished!"

The young farmer stared at his coffee morosely. "Arizona, when you and the other delegates go back, please help us here in the basin. Talk to the Rangers or somebody who can come here and clean up Franklin and his crew of cut-throats. They'll listen to you, won't think you're crazy when you talk about phantom riders and disappearing skeletons."

159

"Don't worry," Ames said. "This will—"

There was a soft scraping noise just outside the window, and Ames spun around. Cameron lifted his head. They both stared at the sight they saw.

Through the hazy, smoke-filmed glass was a pale outline of some terrible demon of Hell, the bare trace of its ethereal being shimmering and its blazing red eyes lancing the fires of perdition from its sockets; it smiled in a wicked leer which seemed to open wide into the black emptiness of death. One bony hand could also be seen, clutching in its shining claw the handle of a Colt revolver.

A revolver whose giant bore was aiming directly for Cameron and Ames.


## VII


Arizona Ames, once again reacting with the cool, perfectly-attuned reflexes of the well-oiled fighting machine he was, threw himself sideways into Gene Cameron just as the sixgun in the skeletal figure's hand spat flame.

The shattering crash of the window glass commingled with the reverberating report of the pistol to fill the room with sound as both the Arizonan and the young nester struck the floor. The bullet thudded into the wall directly behind where the two men had been standing.

Cameron emitted a surprised shout as Ames rolled away from him, fingers digging the .44 from its holster. The intruder fired twice more from the window, and stinging lead ploughed splinters out of the wooden flooring between Ames and Cameron. The Arizonan came into a sitting position, facing the window, and the Colt bucked in his hand, bucked again.

There was a cry of pain from the spectral-dressed form outside and the skull head snapped back and disappeared from view. Ames scrambled to his feet, running for the door. He shouted over his shoulder to the still semi-dazed Cameron, "Outside! There'll be more than one of them!"

Ames jerked open the door and ran onto the porch, his eyes circuiting the darkened farm yard. A flickering glow appeared at the side of the barn off on the left, and the Arizonan dropped flat on the porch as orange fire leaped from the figure's hand and lead ripped into the farmhouse wall behind him. He sighted along his extended right arm and squeezed off two quick shots. The figure retreated behind the barn again.

Cameron came out of the door, with a sixgun in his own hand. He hesitated for a moment, then went to his knees behind a wicker chair to the right of the steps. He was cursing softly, vehemently.

Ames glanced over at him, and as he did he saw an afterglow from around the side of the farmhouse, growing brighter.

"Watch it, Gene," he snapped in warning. "On your right!"

Cameron's head swiveled in that direction, and in that same instant the raider who had fired at them moments earlier came into view, opening up wildly with his sixgun. His left arm hung loosely at his side, and Ames knew his shot through the window had been true to its mark.

The nester dodged out of the way at the sudden volley, moving inadvertently into Ames' line of fire, forcing the cowboy to check the pressure of his finger on the .44's trigger.

Before either of them could recover, the spirit-like form was running across the farm yard in a stumbling, loose-legged gait. Cameron fired after him finlly, missing, and Ames sent two more bullets kicking up dust at the fleeing man's heels. But then he gained the safety of the barn wall, vanishing behind it.

"Damn the luck!" Cameron spat out. "They'll get away now, sure!"

"Maybe not," Ames told him between tightly clenched teeth. "You game for rushing the barn?"

Cameron was already on his feet. "Let's go!"

The two of them ran down off the porch, keeping low and moving in irregular, loping strides. There was no gunfire from the barn. They reached the shadows at its facing wall, moved along it to where they could see around to the rear.

Four of the spirit-like forms were scurrying toward their gleaming mounts hidden in a heavy clump of mesquite and greasewood at the perimeter of the yard.

Ames fanned out away from the barn, leaving Cameron at the corner of the building, and went to one knee in the long shadows along the log-railed fence there.

He emptied the .44 of its final two shots, began to reload quickly as the young farmer continued shooting at the fleeing raiders.

Two of the raiders halted, turning to make a stand; the other two, one of them the wounded one, mounted their horses. The farm yard was alive in bright orange flashes and singing lead and the stench of gunpowder.

Ames had his Colt reloaded now, and he opened up again. He saw one of the raiders firing back at them

162

reel and fall, shouting in surprised agony. The other took one last shot at Cameron and Ames, and then fled to his horse. The three spectral nightriders spurred their mounts forward, the injured one leaning low over the neck of his animal and seeming to be in danger of toppling off. The horse belonged to the one Ames had felled followed behind them, eerily riderless, as they escaped into the night.

Cameron hurried over to where Ames was just standing.

"Let's get our horses and go after 'em!" he shouted.

The Arizonan shook his head, holstering his .44. "By the time we got on their trail, they'd have disappeared."

"But—"

"Come on," Ames told him. "We'll have a look at the one *didn't* get away or disappear. If we're in luck, he won't be more than creased up some."

The nester's face brightened. In his excitement, he had momentarily forgotten about the glowing, unmoving form lying near the clump of mesquite and greasewood some distance away.

"Now maybe we'll get some answers," he said with a thin smile.

They walked quickly to where the fallen figure lay motionless. Ames dropped to one knee beside the man.

One look at the way he was outfitted, and the black cloth mask which covered his head, corroborated a growing conjecture which Ames had had upon hearing Cameron's tale of the ghost killers vanishing when they reached Will Franklin's property, a conjecture which had been born last night during the attack on the train when he had first seen the phantom riders.

The mask was thickly painted with a heavy luminous

dye, more than likely radium based, so as to give it the appearance of a grinning death's-head. There were two small slits for eyeholes. His clothing was all black as well, a lightweight shirt, trousers, leather gloves, heavy boots, and all of it save for the boots had been similarly painted with bone-like designs that would make him, from a distance, resemble a ghostly, skeletal apparition. He also wore, rolled high up on his back and across his shoulders, a thick-weaved black ulster. This garment was unadorned.

Cameron, who had hunkered down beside Ames, said, "Well, I'll be! So that's how they did it!"

The Arizonan nodded, then indicated the rolled ulster. "You see now how they were able to disappear so completely?"

"Sure," the young nester replied swiftly, "They just unrolled those ulsters to that they covered up the painted clothes they had on. Must have stripped off those gloves and took off their masks, too. But what about the horses?"

"Reckon they were also painted up," Ames said. Probably rigged with a rolled-up blanket or the like which could be dropped down over 'em to cover the dye up."

Cameron reached down and stripped the mask from the unconscious killer's head. The man was burly, leather-skinned, mean-looking, with thickly-browed eyes that were set too close together. The Arizonan's bullet had creased a bleeding furrow across his left temple. He was still very much alive.

Cameron said, "I don't know him. Never saw him around these parts before at all."

"More'n likely hired from out of the territory somewhere," Ames guessed.

Cameron was silent for a long moment. Then, slowly, he said, "Listen, Arizona, I'm for riding out to Will Franklin's place right now and calling him down. He's behind this business, sure as hell, and I don't like the idea of Priscilla living under the same roof with him, father or not."

"Maybe he's behind it, and maybe not," Ames said non-committally. "But before we do any confronting, I think we'd best have a talk with this hombre here."

Cameron thought about that, and then conceded that Ames was right. He said, "I'll follow whatever lead you put out, Arizona. I owe you my life after tonight, and I'm not likely to forget or take lightly what you did inside the house."

"We'll bandage that head wound of this coyote's," Ames said, "and take him into Three Rapids to Sheriff McGivern. Maybe we can get to the bottom of this whole thing before the night's out."

He and Cameron lifted the wounded killer and carried him across the farm yard and inside the house. There, the young farmer found some adhesive and gauze wrapping and put a makeshift bandage on the outlaws' head. The man had not regained consciousness.

"There's one thing bothering me, Arizona," Cameron said when they were finished and ready to leave for Three Rapids. "I can't figure it."

"I reckon it's the same thing bothering me," Ames said.

"The reason behind the attack on me tonight?"

The Arizonan nodded. "If it was an attack on you."

"What do you mean?"

"Maybe those bullets were meant for me."

165

# VIII

The thin silver moon hung above the three riders, barely illuminating them. First was Cameron, riding his bay mare; then the outlaw, trussed to the nester's old and swayback plow horse, its halter rope looped around the horn of Cameron's Morgan saddle; finally Ames.

The Arizonan kept keen eyes on both the outlaw and the surrounding land, alert in case the raiders returned to rescue their captured comrade.

The trip from the ranch was slow and plodding, and while the ride to there had taken Arizona Ames the better part of two hours, he calculated the return to Three Rapids would take over three.

Now and then Cameron would speak, cursing the outlaw and his side-kicks, or Franklin, who the nester was convinced was behind the raids. Yet for Ames the answers were still unclear, as hidden as the secret of the ghostly disappearances. But Ames grimly vowed that once the outlaw was behind bars and conscious, the solution would be forthcoming.

Upwards into the Gila Bend mountains the riders climbed, winding through the now all-black boulders and cliffs, the only sound in the still night the clatter of their horses' hooves when they passed over rock. It was past midnight when they entered Three Rapids.

The Golden Pick was still open, but only an occasional loud voice or shout could be heard from its brilliantly lit interior. Other than that and one shining window in the hotel, the town was quiet, asleep.

"The sheriff sleeps inside," Cameron said as they reined in at the office, which was pitch black.

The nester strode to the plank door and began to

166

pound on it with his fists, yelling at the same time for McGivern to wake up. For a long while nothing seemed to stir inside, and Ames had about concluded that Cameron was mistaken, when suddenly a hoarse cry from inside bellowed.

"Aw' right, aw' right, I'm coming!"

Pale yellow glow of a lantern suddenly filled the one dirty window and seeped from beneath the door, and then the door burst open and McGivern stepped out onto the sidewalk in his stocking feet, rubbing his eyes.

"Now, what in hell—" Then he saw Ames and the nester and the firmly tied man. His eyes widened, all sleep disappearing.

"Caught one of the ghosts," Ames explained simply.

McGivern grunted and went to the outlaw. He studied the face for a moment.

"Don't recognize the critter," he said as he lifted the ulster.

Ames had wrapped the outlaw in the garment to keep attention away from them as they rode, but now a portion of the luminous paint gleamed wickedly. "You weren't kiddin'," the sheriff said and dropped the ulster.

"Him and a passel of his buddies tried to kill us at my ranch tonight," Cameron said. "Only Arizona here was a mite quicker and truer with his lead."

"Dead?" the sheriff asked.

"Wounded," Ames replied, "alongside the head."

"Near's the pity," McGivern murmured. "Well, let's get him into the cell then. Cameron, go fetch Doc Moody from the Golden Pick, if'n he ain't too drunk, and bring him around."

167

"Don't mention the reason," Ames cautioned the nester.

"Right," Cameron said and set off on a run for the saloon while Ames and the sheriff untied the outlaw and carried him to the bunk of the jail's one cell.

The man began to moan when they set him down, and he thrashed a bit as he started to regain consciousness. Ames and McGivern stood over him, Ames recounting what had happened and explaining how the clothes made the "ghost" appear and disappear.

"We better strip him of that costume, Ames," the sheriff said, looking down at the wounded outlaw. "Doc Moody will catch one look at that shine and fall over dead away. When he'd stop runnin' every jasper this side of the border would hear tell."

Ames smiled, and began removing the painted clothing. The outlaw was wearing a pair of long johns underneath; the woolen underwear protecting his skin from the dye.

"Leave him like that," McGivern said as he locked away the clothes and boots in a cupboard. "He's not going anywhere tonight."

Suddenly the outlaw's eyes flew open, and after an instant of confusion, he seemed to realize where he was. He tried to jump up and escape, but Ames' strong hands upon his chest and the dizziness of his condition made him fall back. He shut his eyes, his chest heaving with mighty gulps of air.

"What's your name?" Ames asked firmly.

"Stoker . . . Clint Stoker. I—" Then the outlaw clamped his mouth tightly shut. He grinned, now staring up at the Arizonan. "No," he said. "I ain't sayin' no more."

"Stoker," Sheriff McGivern began, anger apparent

in his voice. But then the door burst open again, and Cameron, followed by another man, rushed in. The man was wearing a dirty frock coat and baggy black pants, and in his hands he carried a worn leather satchel bag. His face was red and his eyes blurry, and the long grey-haired mustache drooped down over his mouth.

"In there, Doc," McGivern instructed, and Doc Moody crossed to Stoker.

Ames and the sheriff stood by with their hands resting on their gun butts while the doctor unwound the hastily applied bandages and inspected the deep gash.

"Ain't got nothing on me," Stoker said, wincing as the doctor put some alcohol on the wound.

"No, not much," Cameron retorted angrily. "Only that we caught you red-handed trying to shoot us, and your no-good sidewindin' pal at my window. Yeah, and we got that ghost costume."

The slightly inebriated Doc Moody's hands shook as he took the gauze from his bag.

Stoker caught Doc Moody's timerous nature, and laughed harshly. "Don't let 'em hornswoggle you, Doc," he said. "They'll try and tell you that I came out of a grave, that I'm some old miner that's been long dead." He saw the doctor shudder and he laughed again.

"You've been patchin' horses too long, Moody," McGivern snorted. "He's nothin' but a killer." Angrily he turned to Stoker. "Don't worry, you'll be a ghost afore long. After we stretch that neck of yours a bit."

Stoker blanched, his mouth a white line.

"If that'll be all—" Doc Moody began, nervously flicking his wide-eyed gaze from McGivern to Stoker and then back to the sheriff. He hastily packed his bag, took one last look at the turban he'd fashioned around the outlaw's head, and then scuttled out of the cell.

"I'll be at the Golden Pick if you want me again." Moody's tone indicated he devoutly hoped he wouldn't be summoned again that night. He went out the door, slamming it behind him.

McGivern shook his head. "God knows what he'll be telling the boys at the Golden Pick now. After a few fortifyin' belts, the story will get a little embroidered, and by morning I bet we wouldn't even recognize it."

"I'm sorry," Cameron said. "I got a little hot-headed, hearin' this sidewinder deny what happened."

Ames shrugged. "What's done is done, Gene," he said.

He and McGivern set to work questioning the outlaw, but Stoker wouldn't say anything. Occasionally he would laugh, the grating sound mocking the two men's best efforts, but otherwise his total response was a negative shake of his head. Finally he turned over and feigned sleep.

Cameron by this time was red with fury.

"I'll make that varmint talk," he snapped, stepping with clenched fists to Stoker.

Ames placed a hand on his arm, halting him.

"No, Gene," the Arizonan said. "There are better ways. Now, we're all tired, and nothin' is goin' to get done tonight. Maybe Stoker will be more willin' to talk after he sleeps on it."

Stoker chuckled. "I'll be out of here by tomorrow night, wait and see. This jail ain't going to hold me."

McGivern turned to Ames, saying, "We'd be in

170

bad shape to stop his bunch of raiders if they decide to get him out."

"I'm staying here, then," Ames said.

"Count me in, too," Cameron said. "The three of us ought to be able to hold 'em off a while. The townspeople—"

"Will be under their beds, shiverin'," Stoker hooted.

"If that happens, and you get out, I'll make sure I put a bullet in you before I die," the sheriff vowed.

Ames looked at the old lawman, surprised at the vehemence in his voice, and he was sure McGivern would do as he said.

Ames and Cameron took some extra blankets and curled up on the floor of the office, while the sheriff retired to his cot.

The rest of the night was uneventful, but with the dawn came rude knockings on the door and a demand from some of the locals for information. They had heard via Doc Moody about an all-white specter, swearing he was a dead miner come from the grave.

McGivern, answering the door and the questions, glanced over his shoulder at the sleeping form of Stoker in his dirty pair of long-johns and shook his head. Calmly and firmly he told them no, there wasn't a ghost inside his jail. No, they couldn't come in and tramp around his office. No, he had nothing to say except that Doc had treated a prisoner and everybody knows how Doc likes to tell stories. Then he shut the door and barred it.

"Good idea," Ames said, "not telling anything."

"Way I figure it, until we can get Stoker to tell us who his boss is, it could be any one of them people

171

out there. I let the wrong one in, and we'll lose Stoker for sure."

Cameron went out for coffee and breakfast for the four of them, and when he returned Priscilla Franklin was with him, carrying some of the food.

"Father's in town today, and he heard about the nightrider you brought in," she said as Ames and the sheriff ate. "He wanted to come over and see for himself, but you wouldn't let him in and he came back very angry."

"I can see why," Cameron said. "He wanted in so he could bushwhack us and take Stoker."

"Oh, Gene," Priscilla said miserably, "Are you sure my father is behind all this? Are you really sure?"

"Positive," Cameron said grimly.

"Won't know if'n it's him or somebody else until Stoker talks, M'am," McGivern said. "Don't you get yourself upset until then."

Priscilla began to weep softly, and Cameron put his arm around her shoulder.

"I'm sorry, Pris," he said. "I hope for your sake that I'm wrong, but I just know I'm not."

There was a noise at the window, and the voice of the gambler, Cass Bryce, came through. "Hey, sheriff!"

McGivern went to the window and drew back the heavy muslin curtain. "What is it, Bryce?"

The gambler smiled. "Wanted to find out about this ghost you caught."

"The man I've got is flesh and blood and alive, Bryce. Now go away."

"Now, sheriff, is that any way to treat a member of the citizenry?"

"Maybe not, but that's how I'm treatin' you." He

172

dropped the curtain abruptly, and turned to the Franklin girl. ''Sorry, M'am, but it would be best if you left.''

Priscilla nodded and Cameron opened the door for her. As they exchanged sorrowful glances, Bryce tried to shoulder his way in, jostling Priscilla as he did.

''As I was saying, sheriff—'' he began, and Cameron hit him on the jaw, sending the gambler sprawling on the sidewalk. He sat up, holding his mouth. ''Hey, what—''

Cameron stood ready, fists cocked. ''The sheriff said no.''

''Look, there's a lot of talk going around. Lots of bets to be taken.'' Bryce stood up and slapped the dust from his clothing. ''I need to know just what we have in there. I could lose a great deal of money if I made the wrong move.''

''Make another move like you just did,'' McGivern said, ''and you might lose more than money.''

Bryce opened his mouth to say something, saw the hard glint in the sheriff's, Cameron's and Ames' eyes, and shut it again. He pivoted on his heel and stalked away.

Back inside the office, Ames said, ''It's about time to see if Stoker is more willing to talk, I'd say.''

It proved not to be. The outlaw was as stubbornly silent as he had been the night before. He gloated that they were wasting their time, that he wasn't about to talk and ruin his chances of being sprung. Disgusted and frustrated, the three of them returned to the office.

''He's not going to talk,'' McGivern said, slumping in a chair, ''not so long as he figgers he's going to be free.''

''Tomorrow night, he said,'' Cameron snapped. ''Out by then, he bet us. The way he talked about it,

Bryce wouldn't have taken the odds against him. Damn!''

Ames stood near the cupboard, deep in thought. He rolled a cigarette and smoked it, rubbing his chin and the bridge of his nose. He had the portent that the tomorrow night—this very night, now—was more important than the mere bragging of a desperado.

It was, as Cameron implied, in the tone and manner of his voice, as if he knew there was more brewing. That meant it was more vital than ever to prod Stoker into a confession. Yet normal means would not work . . .

He took a deep breath and said, ''Perhaps we can trick him, sheriff.''

''Trick Stoker?'' McGivern frowned. ''I don't follow.''

''I have a plan,'' Ames said, smiling wryly.

## IX

Arizona Ames moved stealthily along the rear of the tin-roofed jail, his .44 unholstered and cocked at ready in his right hand. He felt hot and uncomfortable, but grimly determined, inside the heavy black, luminous-dyed clothing which had belonged to the killer Clint Stoker; the death's-head mask was tight around his head. He hoped none of the townspeople were about to see his dancing, spectral movements through the shadows, and he hoped fervently that his plan would work. If it didn't—

Ames put the thought out of his mind. There was no use in ancitipating more trouble than already abounded. He made his way as silently as possible toward the barred window at the far end of the adobe-walled building, through which shone a pale light from the lantern on the sheriff's desk inside.

When he reached the window, he keened his ears for some sound from within the cell, but there was none. He reasoned that Stoker was lying on his cot, which was located in such a position so as to afford him a view of the window. The outlaw hadn't been asleep minutes earlier, when Sheriff McGivern had given Ames the go-ahead. There was no reason to assume that he was sleeping now.

The Arizonan raised his head cautiously, bringing the .44 up in front of him until his eyes and the muzzle of the Colt were on a level with the sill of the barred rectangle. Then he straightened up all the way, framing the glowing death's head in the window and poking the gun through the bars. He made as much noise as he could, just in case Stoker was doing or looking in another direction.

But the outlaw had been lying on his back, gazing up at the window. When he saw the ghostly head appear, the sixgun, he cried out in fear and surprise and rolled scrambling off the cot. Ames fired twice with the .44, purposely aiming wide so that both bullets thudded into the cotton wadding of the cot's mattress. Stoker was backed against the cell door now, crouching like a cornered animal, his eyes bulging wide with liquid terror.

He was screaming for the sheriff in a high-pitched whine, but McGivern by prearrangement had stepped out onto the porch in front after announcing he needed a touch of fresh air.

Ames fired again, missing high by design, although he made it appear as if the shot was hurried due to circumstance. He drew the Colt back then, ducking down and away from the window. He ran quickly along the shadows at the rear of the jail, pulling off the death's-head mask as he did so. He could hear Stoker yelling inside the cell.

When he reached the side of the building, McGivern was there. The sheriff's own Colt was unholstered and in his hand. He grinned some around his perpetual plug of tobacco, nodded to Ames, and then raised his sixgun high over his head. He began yelling at the top of his voice, squeezing off four shots in rapid succession into the night sky.

Ames slipped into the open side door of the mercantile store as he did so; that was where he had changed moments earlier. He took off the spectral garb, folding it into the black ulster which he had worn high across his shoulders. He put his own clothing back on, strapped the black carved cartridge belt-and-holster onto his hip, and went to the door, listening.

There was a small commotion outside as some of the townspeople, attracted by the shooting, gathered to find out what was happening. McGivern told them it was nothing and dispersed them rapidly. Silence settled beyond the door.

After a moment, there was a soft knock and the sheriff eased inside the mercantile store to join Ames.

"Nice shootin'," McGivern commented. "Stoker's still screaming fit to be tied. I reckon maybe this scheme of yours'll work after all, Ames."

"Let's hope so," Ames said.

"You figure enough time's passed by now, or do we let Stoker stew in his own juice a mite longer?"

"If he's going to talk, it'll be while he's still plenty shaken. We'd best go in now."

McGivern nodded, and the two men hurried around

176

to the front of the jail and went inside. Stoker stood gripping the bars of his cell with bloodless fists. His face was bone-white in the lantern glare, and his eyes were still fear-widened.

McGivern looked over at him. "They got away, Stoker. I'd say you're danged lucky you ain't dead."

"Maybe he won't be so lucky next time," Ames said, resting a hip at the edge of the sheriff's cluttered desk so that he was facing the frightened outlaw.

"What you mean, next time?" Stoker demanded.

"These pals of your want you silenced up for good, no mistake about that," McGivern said. "They ain't going to stop at one miss."

"They—they wouldn't kill me." Stoker's voice was uncertain, tremulous.

Ames pressed the advantage. "No? What do you figure tonight was all about?"

"Just a warning, that's all."

"What kind of warning?"

"To keep my mouth shut."

The sheriff snorted. "You're a bigger fool than you look, Stoker. That ghost pard of yours pitched three slugs into your cell with you just now. That don't sound like no warning I ever heard of. You ask me, he was trying to ventilate your hide good and proper."

"They want you dead, Stoker, face up," Ames said coldly. "Dead men keep secrets no live ones can."

"They know I wouldn't talk!"

"Then why'd they try to kill you tonight?"

"I—" Stoker was trying to convince himself that Ames and the sheriff were wrong, that he was in no danger from his compatriots. It was a losing battle. Fear was beginning to win out over whatever loyalties he had, fear and anger at the purported inequity which had been attempted against him.

It was very silent in the jail. Ames was breathing softly, waiting and tensed, and McGivern's jaws had ceased their rhythmic chewing of the plug in his mouth. Finally Stoker moistened his lips and said haltingly, "Listen, you got to protect me. You got to put a guard outside. If they come back . . ."

"We don't have to do nothing at all," the sheriff told him calmly. "Far as we're concerned, them pards of yours can have you. You ain't any use to us."

Stoker's face blanched even whiter. "You don't mean that!"

"Hell if I don't," McGivern said.

"But you got to protect me! You're the law!"

McGivern snorted again and looked at Ames. "You see how they cry law and justice when it suits 'em, Ames?"

The Arizonan nodded.

"The sheriff's right," he said to Stoker. "Unless you give us some cooperation, help us get these so-called friends of yours, we'd just as soon you had their justice as ours."

"Another thing, too, Stoker," McGivern added. "You help us, and maybe you'll cheat a hangman's rope. We'll put in a word for you at your trial. You don't help us and you're a dead man either way. By a rope or by a bullet. You think about that, Stoker."

Stoker thought about it. He thought about it hard. Sweat coated his forehead, and his hands clasped and unclasped the iron bars. Ames and McGivern knew that it was just a matter of time now, that they had succeeded in their plan to get the outlaw to talk. But they didn't speak, waiting; to further badger his would be to invite the possibility of belligerance and continued silence.

After several minutes had passed, Stoker said in a choked voice, "They deserve whatever happens to 'em! The dirty sidewinders had no call to throw down on me! I'm no rat, and they knew that! They had no call!"

"You want to tell us about it now?" Ames asked softly.

"Yeah," Stoker said. Anger had replaced most of his fear now, and his white cheeks were splotched with red. "Yeah, I'll tell you about it, all right. I'll tell you everything I know. They deserve what happens to 'em after what they tried to do to me tonight."

"Suppose we start with who's back of these supposed ghost raids around Three Rapids," McGivern said.

Stoker shook his head. "I dunno who it is. I never saw him. None of us did. We got our orders written out and left at a drop point out near the cemetery."

Ames and the sheriff looked at one another, then at Stoker. Was the outlaw telling the truth? They decided mutely that he was. He had no reason to hold back anything now that he had decided to spill all.

Stoker went on: "But there was supposed to be a big meet of some kind tonight. To divvy up the money we got from the train, I think. It was in the orders we picked up tonight, along with the ones telling us to gun you and that nester Cameron out at his place."

Ames was suddenly excited. "Where's this meeting to be?"

"At the cemetery."

"What time?"

"Midnight."

179

McGivern consulted a gold pocket watch. "Past eleven now," he said.

The Arizonan said quickly to the outlaw. "Suppose you tell us how you manage to disappear in that graveyard? What's the secret of Superstition Cemetery?"

"That big crypt at one end," Stoker told him. "There's a secret entrance to it, around to the rear. The whole wall slides up, and there's plenty enough room for men and horses both to pass through."

The sheriff whistled softly.

"So that's it!" he exclaimed. "Now who would have figured such a thing?"

"The old miner who built it was queer for secret passages and the like, the way we heard it," Stoker said. "When he had the crypt built, he made sure to have that hidden entrance put into it."

Ames frowned slightly, considering.

"That crypt's too small to keep a dozen men and horses," he said. "There must be a passageway or something leading underground from inside. That's the only answer."

"Sure," the outlaw confirmed. "I told you that old miner was queer for stuff like that. The whole platform where his coffin is swings out when you work a hand lever hidden on one side. There's a ramp leading down into an old mine shaft, plenty wide. Hell, that whole section is honeycombed with underground shafts and passageways. The old miner owned the claim to the area, and had the crypt built right on top of all the mine tunneling."

Ames had an idea. "Is there still gold veins in those shafts? That would explain one reason why whoever's behind this wouldn't want the cemetery—and the tunneling, too, covered up by flood waters of the Sangre River Dam.''

But Stoker shook his head. "There nary an ounce of the yaller stuff in those shafts any more. It was all played out ten years back, plain enough."

McGivern, whose eyes were bright at the tale being related by the outlaw, said, "You say the whole section under the graveyard is honeycombed with these mine shafts. Which one of 'em's going to house that meeting tonight?"

"There's a big grotto at the end of the main shaft under the crypt," Stoker told him. "Got lanterns and supplies and cots in there. That's where we been stayin' since we was hired out of New Mexico territory, when we wasn't pulling those crazy ghost raids."

Ames asked the outlaw the exact locations of the hidden levers to open the entrance in the crypt, and to operate the platform leading to the underground ramp. Then, when Stoker had told him, he stood up from the desk and motioned to McGivern.

"I reckon we've got enough now, sheriff," he said.

"Reckon we do at that."

They started across to the door. Behind them, Stoker shouted "Hey! Hey, you're not gonna leave me here alone, are you? You promised me protection if I talked?"

"Don't you worry none, Stoker," McGivern said over his shoulder. "You'll get everything what's coming to you."

He and Ames went out onto the jail porch; there, he examined his pocket watch again.

"Half past now," he said. "We ain't got much time, Ames."

181

"Not enough to round up a proper posse quietly," the Arizonan agreed.

"Why quietly?"

"We still don't know who's behind all this, sheriff. If word got out to the wrong parties, we might not find anybody at the graveyard when we got there. Or worse, we'd ride right into an ambush."

McGivern nodded. "See what you mean. But say, maybe there is a way to round up a posse quiet like. Vern Douglas is usually over to the hotel having himself a late snack this time of night. I use him sometimes as a deputy when I'm away from Three Rapids. We can send him around to gather up all the ranchers and nesters and townfolk he can locate—only tellin' 'em enough so's they'll ride along with him."

"Good," Ames said. Let's talk to Douglas, and then you and me'll ride out to the graveyard to wait for the posse. If we hurry, we can get out there not much past midnight."

Ames and McGivern found Vern Douglas in the hotel dining room, told him quietly what they wanted him to do. Douglas left immediately. The sheriff and Ames then went back to the jail and picked up their horses and rode out of town at a full gallop.

To what both men hoped would be the showdown that would put an end, once and for all, to the ghost killers of Superstition Cemetery.

## X

Superstition Cemetery was quiet; a deep, foreboding kind of silence hung like a black pall over the graves. Its stones and wooden crosses stood out of the earth and grasses—and above all loomed the murky pale marble home of Jedediah Harrison's mortal remains.

His crypt seemed to overshadow the rest of the burial grounds, sucking into its core the sounds of the living, making the chirrups of crickets and tree frogs and even the whisper of the night breeze unheard, un-natural, as if in a vacuum.

Ames and the sheriff stood uneasily in the shadows of some cotton woods, both knowing that in spite of their intelligence and common sense therewas an aura present which couldn't be denied.

They had ridden to the cemetery at a hard gallop, dismounting and walking their horses to the trees when they neared, just in case a guard had been posted. Now, after circling around and downwind to the grave-yard, they waited and watched. They had seen the soft glow of a cigarette from one of the markers; an in-dication that a guard was on duty, and that the pre-cautions Ames and McGivern had taken were all to the good.

The cigarette glowed again, and there was a slight scuffling sound as the guard changed positions. Ames spotted the black figure as he stood and stretched. Then the shadow was gone, melting in with the other obscurations. The Arizonan nudged the sheriff.

"I'm going to sneak around behind him. You keep me covered, and if he sees me, shoot to kill."

McGivern nodded and hunkered down, pistol ready and aimed at the vicinity of the guard. Ames slowly, toe-and-heel, inched his way around the perimeter of the cemetery.

The glow told him that the guard was facing the trees, and the merest rustling noise, the slightest sweep of grass, would call his attention to Ames. There was one section of bare ground which the cowboy crawled through, using the cover of the stones as much as possible. Then he was on the other side of the crypt to the guard and was able to move a little more freely.

The stone of the markers was cold and alien in Ames' fingers as he wound his way through them, feeling his way before stepping down hard, occasionally taking the time to clear the brittle twigs and dry leaves from his path.

The guard's silhouette became clearer, the inkiness of his ulster-covered costume shades darker than the surrounding black night and grey stones. Then Ames was within a half-dozen graves from the guard, then four, then two . . .

Ames' heel caught a pebble, and the small rock hit the base of a marker. The slight sound made the guard stiffen and he began to turn. Ames had to act fast. If the guard didn't fire, the sheriff would, and either way the alarm would be sounded, warning the others. Ames leaped through the air, hurtling the last two grave stones in a giant leap, and tackled the shrouded guard high in the chest, sending both of them to the ground.

The guard had started, "Hey, what—" But then the wind had been forced from his lungs by Ames' swift attack, and he hit the dirt without another sound. He was big and muscular, his arm tightening around Ames in a bear hug, his legs trying to come up to maim the Arizonan.

Ames rolled to one side and brought his arm across the guard's throat, then rolled back on top, choking the man. The ulster hampered the guard, and for all his brutality, he was no match for the Arizonan.

Ames stood in a half crouch and delivered two bone-cracking jabs to the guard, one in the stomach, the

184

other on the aw. The guard sagged, unconscious. He was dragged unceremoniously through the grass and graves to the cottonwoods. There he was trussed securely with rope, gagged, and firmly secured to one of the tree trunks. He squirmed, but the knots held; and he wouldn't be free until he was collected later by the law.

"Or his friends," Sheriff McGivern said in a low voice as he and Ames walked back to the crypt. "There's only two of us right now, and if we make the wrong move—"

The certain awareness of what would follow a wrong move was left unsaid, though both men knew it would mean at least two more bodies for the ground of Superstition Cemetery.

Outwardly, the large tomb of the rich miner looked impregnable. The marble slabs were fitted tightly; the one huge iron door was corroded and locked, sealed against entrance; and not a window was there, barred or not.

At the back, where the prisoner, Stoker, had said there was a secret entrance, McGivern felt the smooth stone and whispered, "I remember when this was built. Just before the gold began to give out around these parts. But then old Jed was always one to time things right. He got sick, knew he was going to die soon, so he sent all the way to St. Louis for the marble and workmen. Wouldn't have any of the local men work on it; kept everything a big secret. At the time, nobody knew why. Now I do, what with all these passages and everything."

Ames was busy reconnoitering the area, searching for the thin lever which was supposed to operate the wall. "Still seems odd to me why a dyin' man would

185

go to all this trouble. He wouldn't be around to reap the rewards."

"Old Jed was a strange one," McGivern explained. "Always talking about bein' buried alive, on account of a mining accident when he was a button. He was caught in a cave-in for five days, I heard tell, along with eight others. He was the only one who lived. I guess that can change a man some."

"So he was afraid of having it done to him again," Ames replied. "And I bet he filled those tunnels with food and water and made sure it was a secret so that others wouldn't steal from him. I wonder how this was discovered, considerin'—"

Ames paused, his hands groping in the darkness. "I think I found it." He showed the sheriff what he was holding. "See here? This carved figure?"

The sheriff studied the column of bas-relief etchings which adorned the support pillars at each corner of the crypt. "You mean that miner carved there? The one like on his plaque?" McGivern asked, peering closer.

"Yes. His pick is loose I can move it downward like this. I think that—" Ames pressed against the pick handle, and from deep inside there came a soft rumbling, grating noise, a sound similar to a miniature earthquake or cave-in.

Both Ames and the sheriff had expected for the wall to lift up, just as Stoker had explained. Yet neither really comprehended the mechanical genius which had designed the secret entrance.

Somewhat in awe, they stood back and watched as the complete rear wall slowly tilted on some unseen axis and without a hesitant motion, rose as one solid piece. At its peak, when the wall was parallel with the earth, there was a sharp click and it stopped.

186

Ames said, "It will close in a few seconds, according to Stoker. I'm going inside. You wait here for the posse."

"But—"

"It has to be done, sheriff. We don't know what's down there, and we could be sending half the men in the basin to their death if the tunnels and rooms are booby-trapped or well guarded. In places like that, many men can be worse than too few."

With that, the lean Arizonan slipped inside the crypt, and not a moment too soon. Almost on his heels the great slab of marble began to lower, sealing him inside.

The interior was pitch black. Ames felt his way to the bier in the middle of the room, and there he struck a wooden match. The crypt was bare, absolutely without any kind of decoration of carving save for the giant coffin on its stone pedestal. The bier looked as formidable and solid as the crypt itself had seemed, the stone top a full seven foot by three foot and six inches thick. Then the light went out.

Ames lit another match and after a minute found the hidden lever on the bier which operated its mechanism. He tugged on the lever then stood back, unholstering his .44 just in case there was somebody waiting on the other side.

The same near silent rumbling sound emitted from the tomb, and then it began to swing back on one corner, not stopping until it rested against the far wall.

It was like opening a cavern to hell. A wide, stone-hewn ramp led downward from where Arizona Ames stood by the bier. The ramp was lost against the rough flooring. Still with gun in hand, Ames slowly worked his way down the slope, and when the last of his matches went out, he continued in the dark.

The ramp, wide enough for horses and riders, gently leveled out, and though Ames could not see how high the roof of the tunnel was, he could tell it was over arm's length.

A rider, hunched over his mount, could pass through here, he thought, and once the passages were lit with firebrands, the way would be clear for the galloping hordes of "ghost" killers to come and go quickly.

The tunnel walls were rough and sharp against Ames' free hand. He cut his palm on the edges of rock as he slowly made his way along the passage. He stumbled once on the similarly jagged floor surface; the sound of his boots echoed faintly down the unseen corridors.

Stoker had been right about this being a mining tunnel, for there was no attempt at smoothing the sides, and the shoring was still open and bare.

It seemed to the Arizonan to take hours to traverse the black shaft, for he was forced to take as much time here as when he was sneaking up on the guard. Again, he scraped the skin from his hand, adding another bleeding cut to his scratched and bruised skin.

The gallery twisted and turned like an angry river bed, making Ames loose his way and fumble for the sides.

Then, as Ames turned one especially sharp corner, he saw a faint glow ahead, like the mingling of a thousand fireflies.

He stepped a little faster, now having a point by which he could be guided, and as he neared the wavering sparks, they began to take form, to become steadier and brighter, and he knew that he was entering the den of the "ghost" killers.

He heard the first low murmurs of voices, and once

188

a gruff bellow of laughter, sharply cut off by another's swearing.

He edged closer, mind and ears keenly alert, his eyes on the scintillation before him. There was another very wide curve, and then he stopped.

He backed against the wall, pressing himself closer to the gloom.

Just ahead of him was a big grotto, a hollowed-out room about a hundred feet long on all sides. It was lit by two lanterns which were in niches along the walls; their glow adding to the radiance of the men grouped around the large, thick wood table. The table was in the middle of the large grotto; the killers in their ghost costumes.

Ames counted eleven "ghosts" and at the head of the table was a specter, but completely draped in a white hood and shift. Only two eye holes and the man's hands resting on the table were other than the material he was wearing.

Ames couldn't tell the masked person's identity. But he knew that there was the leader, the boss, of the cut-throat crew of raiders.

Around the grotto were barrels and boxes of supplies, and on the table were empty canvas bags. They were khaki colored and on their front was the printed emblem of the Territory. They were, Ames figured, the sacks the Sangre Dam money had been shipped in.

A deep, throbbing fury began to well in the Arizonan's chest, making his muscles tighten and his hands ball into fists. He took a step closer, almost angry enough to go in alone, shooting as many as he could before he was cut down. Only the thought that Sheriff McGivern was above him, waiting for the

189

posse, which for all he knew had already arrived, kept him still.

Suddenly a gravel-throated voice snapped at him from behind. "Grab sky, stranger," it commanded, "or you're dead."

Ames froze, feeling the cold dull barrel of a large-bore gun hit his spine. Somewhere along the passage he had passed a hidden guard, probably concealed in one of the many niches and cul-de-sacs. He was prodded forward until he was standing at the entrance of the grotto, in full view of the now alerted raiders. He was defenseless and trapped, and Arizona Ames tensed his body, half expecting a piece of lead to come shattering through him right then and there.

The outlaws all began to talk at once. Then came the voice of the white-hooded figure, who ordered silence.

"Quiet!" he shouted, and after the outlaws had toned down, he said to the guard behind Ames, "Take his gun."

The guard grabbed the .44 out of Ames' hand, making sure that the slightest protest on the Arizonan's part would lead to a quick bullet in the back.

Ames thought he recognized the voice of the leader, and as he considered it, he was suddenly sure beyond a shadow of a doubt. It belonged to the man he had suspected as might having been behind the raids and killings, as one who would profit greatly by such actions and the delay in the building of the Sangre River Dam.

It belonged to the banker, Neal P. Celtas.

## XI

"So you're the coyote behind all this, Celtas," Arizona Ames said with thinly controlled anger, his hands clenched into fists at his sides.

There was a brief moment of silence, and then the pudgy little banker said, "So you recognized my voice, eh, Ames? Well, all right, then. I guess there's no more purpose to be served in my little disguise, now that you've let the cat out of the bag."

With those words, Celtas reached up and removed the white hood amidst murmurs from the assembled outlaws.

Celtas was smiling, and it was a cold and evil curving of his lips. There was a big .41 caliber Colt Frontier revolver that appeared to be the size of a cannon in his small fist.

"Bring him in, Garth," he said to the raider who had captured Ames. "Now that he's found out our secret little hideaway, he'll have to pay the consequences. And I think I'll attend to that little chore myself."

Garth prodded the Arizonan from behind into the center of the lantern-lit grotto, where Celtas and the hired raiders were grouped around the wooden table containing the empty money sacks.

Celtas stepped up to him and waved the .41 Frontier under Ames' nose. He was very brave with almost a dozen other guns to back him up.

"How'd you find out about the crypt, Ames?" he demanded. "And about the meeting in the grotto here tonight?"

The Arizonan said nothing, his lips compressed into a bloodless line and his steady gray eyes meeting the crooked banker's unblinkingly.

"From Stoker, I'll bet," one of the hired raiders said. "I knew he'd spill his guts to the law! We shoulda made sure he was dead before we left that nester's place last night!"

"Never mind, never mind," Celtas said. He was still staring into Ames' eyes, and the Arizonan was still returning the fiery glare levelly. "Who else knows about these shafts, Ames? Who else came here with you tonight?"

"I rode out by myself," Ames said. "But McGivern knows. He's out rounding up a posse right now. They'll be here within the hour."

He wanted Celtas to know that the sheriff and the local inhabitants were on to the use of Superstition Cemetery for the nocturnal raiders' hideout, but not that McGivern was waiting outside or that the posse was surely by this time almost to the graveyard. He got the reaction he had hoped for.

"Well, that's just fine," Celtas said. "We'll be gone from here in another ten minutes, and by the time that posse gets here there won't be a trace of me or any of my men. And nobody but you could possibly know that I conceived this entire scheme."

"McGivern knows that, too," Arizona Ames lied.

"I don't think so," Celtas said shrewdly. "I don't think so at all. No, you're the only one, Ames." He chuckled suddenly, a high-pitched, almost feminine sound. "Things couldn't have worked out better, as a matter of fact, not even if I'd planned them this way."

"The money the boys took off the train the other night has already been divvied up, and as soon as they perform one more little task for me they'll be riding back to New Mexico, where they came from. And the posse will be out here prowling around while they're performing that task, so they won't be hindered in any way."

"What are you having them do, Celtas?" Ames wanted to know.

"Why, blow up the damsite," the banker said with another high-pitched chuckle. "Bury that construction area under rock and debris that'll take six months to clear away, the explosion will. By that time, I'll be the richest man in this section of the country, because the country will still want that dam built, in spite of the delay."

Celtas' eyes gleamed. "When Arizona achieves statehood one day, I may even run for governor. What do you think of that, Ames? Neal P. Celtas—Governor of the Sovereign State of Arizona!"

Ames repressed a shudder of disgust. He had to stall for time now, keep this obvious egomaniac talking as long as possible to give the posse time to reach Superstition Cemetery.

He said softly, "How do you figure to be so rich, Celtas? What's behind all these raids and this sabotage of the Sangre River Dam project?"

"Haven't you guessed by now?" Celtas' words were mocking.

Ames had, but to pretend ignorance was to gain that precious time.

"No," he said. "I haven't."

"Well, I'll tell you then. The Southeastern Cattleman's Exchange and Trust Bank owns the mortgages on the property of ninety-five percent of the small landowners in the Gila Basin. The construction of the Sangre River Dam will enable them to pay off those

193

mortgages, to prosper; the land hereabouts will be productive and fertile with the proper irrigation and flood control that the dam will give it. Land in the Gila Basin will be worth a fortune when that dam's built!''

"So by stopping the project for six months to a year, you hope to drive the settlers off their land, foreclosing on their mortgages and then buying up the property at next to nothing under a series of phony names."

"Precisely," Celtas said. There was a warped pride in his voice. "And it'll work, too. The ghost raids have everyone in this area plenty scared. Most of the small landowners are only remaining because of the prospect of the dam's immediate creation. One or two, in fact, have already defaulted and moved out."

"The rest won't be able to last out a year without the sure construction of the Sangre River Dam. Before erection begins at long last, I will have refused them extensions on their loans in my capacity as president of the bank, and foreclosed. When the dam is finally completed, I will own a large percentage of the fertile land in the Gila Basin."

"What about the large landowners like Franklin?" Ames asked. "They won't be driven out by a delay in the dam's construction. In fact, they don't want the dam to be built at all."

"Franklin is the only one of these with whom I'm concerned. The others are less stubborn and less resistant to the right kind of pressure. And I'm not worried about Franklin in the slightest," Celtas added with a secret smile. "After tonight, he won't be a problem at all."

"What's that supposed to mean?" the Arizonan demanded.

"I've arranged it with the boys here to plant some incriminating evidence on Franklin's property after they've blown up the damsite—some of the dynamite, and a ghost outfit or two. Why do you suppose I've had them ride over Franklin's property, making sure Cameron and some of the other nesters saw them disappear there?"

"To throw suspicion onto Franklin as being behind the ghost raids and killings, or at least fully involved." Arizona Ames' voice was cold and hard.

"Exactly. When that incriminating evidence is discovered, McGivern will have to arrest Franklin as being responsible. That's the reason I've kept after that old fool to do something, hoping he'd settle on Franklin as the prime suspect."

Celtas moistened his lips. "After Franklin is tried and hung, his holdings will revert to his daughter. I don't anticipate any difficulty in persuading her to sell out to me—at a mere percentage of the land's actual value, of course."

"Why did you try to have Gene Cameron and me killed last night, Celtas?"

"You, because you were getting too nosy, Ames," the banker replied. "I suspected you from the first. I wanted you out of the way before you found out something important. So when you asked McGivern directions to Cameron's place in the hotel, I knew you were going out there and I saw the chance of taking care of you both at the same time."

"Why did you want Cameron dead?"

"Because of Franklin's daughter, of course, She

loves him. With him dead, and her father in jail for murder, she won't want to remain in the Gila Basin will she? She'll sell out the moment I ask her.''

"Then Cameron's still marked for a bullet?''

"Naturally. And he'll get one tonight, after the dam site is blown up. As for you, Ames, I'm afraid that you're going to get yours right now . . .''

Ames knew that the time for stalling was over. Even though the posse hadn't arrived as yet, he had to make some kind of move to save his own life and he had to make it right at that moment. There was a kill light in Celtas' eyes, and his finger was tight on the trigger of the Colt Frontier.

The Arizonan lashed out with the sudden swiftness of a striking diamondback with the toe of his right boot, catching Celtas on the shinbone. The banker emitted a high, thin scream of pain, and the gun in his hand wavered as his full concentration was momentarily centered on the agony in his leg.

Ames swept his right hand up, fingers closing over the barrel of the weapon and jerking it out of Celtas' hand.

Then the cowboy pivoted to the side, raising his right leg high and pistoning it against the wooden table, upending it with flying money sacks into the group of surprise-frozen nightriders. Ames jumped back, and fired twice from the hip with deadly, swift accuracy.

There were two almost simultaneous explosions of glass as the Arizonan's bullets sent the two lanterns in the grotto spinning out of their niches to shatter on the rock floor. The cavern was suddenly plunged into complete darkness, save for the ghostly luminosity of the radium-dyed clothing worn by the outlaws.

Celtas was still screaming in pain, and there were

confused shouts from the hired raiders, as Ames raced for the shaft in which he had been captured and which led upward to the crypt. He tried to remember the turns and loops in the absolute black, and was only partially successful. He slammed into one of the rocky protuberances which jutted out from the wall as he tried too quickly to feel his way along, tearing his shirt and opening a bleeding gash in his left arm.

Ames started to move around the protuberance, then heard scurrying noises behind him and turned to look back at the way he had come. He saw the flickering glow of the ghostly outfits as the raiders, having recovered, began to pursue him.

Ames braced himself with his feet wide apart and sent two slugs down the passageway just as two of the spectral figures loomed into view. One of them half-turned with a bullet high in his chest and toppled soundlessly to the shaft's floor. The other snapped a wild shot at the Arizonan, and then retreated hurriedly.

Ames spun around and began to run upward again, his guiding hands on the side wall being cut and scraped in a dozen more places by sharp edges of rock. He had only seconds at best, and if the bier platform had been levered closed by the outlaw who had captured him, he was done for; he did not know where the lever to operate the platform was located on this side.

But the platform was still swiveled wide, and Ames let out a whistling breath as he neared the ramp. There was just enough grayness in the black to show him the opening in the crypt. He reached the ramp and scrambled up it and gained the crypt's stone floor.

His hand sought and located immediately the lever to swing the platform closed, and he jerked it up.

Rumbling, it began to swivel shut—and none too soon. Skeletal dancing light illuminated the ramp up which Arizona Ames had just climbed as the raiders came into view in the shaft below; two or three shots, all missing badly, echoed loudly in the confined space. The Arizonan thought he could hear Celtas' high-pitched voice shouting at the outlaws to hurry, to get Ames before he escaped.

The cowboy was already racing across the blackened crypt before the bier platform had fully swung closed. He located the entrance wall, and felt frantically along it, looking for the lever which would open it from the inside, cursing himself for not having gotten the information from Stoker before leaving Three Rapids.

Precious seconds ticked by. Sweat broke out on Ames' forehead. He looked over his shoulder and his chest. The platform was swinging open again. Celtas and his hired raiders had activated the lever from the passageway below.

Ames knew that he was a dead man if he didn't get that wall opened within the next thirty seconds. Feverishly, his bleeding hands scurried over every inch of the smooth marble of the wall—and then just when it seemed too late, he found the lever! It was located in a small recess in the stone, almost at floor level. The Arizonan jerked it sharply downward, and instantly the entire wall began to slide up.

Ames waited only long enough for a two-foot open space to appear at the bottom. Then he threw himself flat and rolled under the wall, out into the lighter black of the night. He was on his feet and running immediately, heading for the nearest gravestone which would afford him cover. The wall was all the way up now, and Celtas and the outlaws were in the crypt, charging across it, firing at the Arizonan's back.

Ames left his feet in a headlong dive as he approached one of the wide granite epitaphs, twisting his body behind the protective stone as more shots echoed behind him, destroying the stillness of the night. Where was McGivern? Ames thought frantically. Where was the posse? The outlaws had all spilled out of the crypt now, were fanning out; Celtas knew there were only two bullets left in that Colt Frontier . . .

Suddenly, there were several other shots and a coldly shouted, authoritative command from off in the darkness to the left. It was the voice of Sheriff Abe McGivern, and one of the most welcome sounds Arizona Ames had ever heard.

It said: "All right, boys! Drop your irons, every one of 'em, or we'll cut you down where you stand!"

There was surprised confusion among the ranks of the outlaws. Several of them opened fire finally, sending a volley of lead in the direction of the voice, and then all hell broke loose. The night erupted in brilliant muzzle flashes from the left and the right of the crypt.

Four of the raiders fell instantly, wounded or dead; others tried to scurry back inside the crypt, trying to open the wall which had already slid closed again, and were cut down by the relentless fire. The remainder threw down their guns and raised their hands high, clustering into a small circle of surrender. The shooting stopped as quickly as it had begun.

Ames saw Neal Celtas sneaking along the far side of the crypt, and sent the last two bullets in the Frontier high into the wall above his head. Celtas froze, his face white with terror, and put his pudgy hands up.

Ames went over there and shoved the now-tremblin[ɡ] banker up to the wall, frisking him for other weapon[s]. He had none.

The Arizonan stepped back, and as he did s[o] McGivern materialized out of the night. Ames coul[d] see two dozen men coming up from their concealmen[t] to take care of the remaining outlaws, among the[m] Vern Douglas, Gene Cameron, Will Franklin, an[d] even three or four of the territorial delegates.

McGivern looked at the cowering banker and sai[d] scornfully, "So you're the sidewinder behind all thi[s], eh, Celtas? I never did much cotton to you. Too dange[r], pushy, too danged eager."

"You old fool!" Celtas returned shakily. "If [it] hadn't been for this meddling Ames, I'd have su[c]ceeded in my plan! You never would have caug[ht] me!"

McGivern smiled. "Maybe, maybe not. But you'[re] caught now, ain't you, Celtas? And that's all th[at] matters."

He turned to the Arizonan. "Sorry we didn't ope[n] up on them nightriders soon as you come out of th[e] crypt, Ames. But it all happened too fast, you rolli[n] out like that, that we couldn't be sure it was you [or] not."

Ames grinned wearily. "I'm just thankful yo[u] opened up when you did. I figured I was a goner."

"So did we," the sheriff admitted. "Posse got he[re] more'n ten minutes ago, and some of the boys wante[d] to go in right away. But I told 'em you was in ther[e] and so they went along with waiting until you com[e] out—or them killers did."

Just then, Gene Cameron and Will Franklin cam[e]

up to where Ames and McGivern were standing. McGivern said wryly, "Seems like Cameron here was out to Franklin's place, accusing him of being behind the ghost raids, when Vern Douglas rode up with the posse."

"I guess I owe Mr. Franklin an apology," the young nester said with humility. "I went off half cocked, accusing him without any definite proof."

"Reckon I misjudged you a mite, too, Cameron," Franklin said gruffly. "You got more spine than I figured; you handled yourself right well tonight."

"Well thanks, Mr. Franklin," Cameron grinned, and that grin was infectious.

McGivern and Franklin smiled slowly, then widely, and as tired as he was, Ames felt his own mouth turning upward at the corners. He had the feeling that everything was going to work out just fine from now on. The territorial money would be recovered in short order, the construction of the Sangre River Dam would soon begin, and there would be no more terrorism from Neal Celtas and his Ghost Killers of Superstition Cemetery.

Although he was too humble a man to think such thoughts, Arizona Ames had done his homeland, his Governor, and himself proud.


## XII


The ceremony was held in the morning, before the heat of the day wilted the festivities. The sun was just over the top of the Gila Bend mountains, a yellow blaze in a light blue setting, making the waters of Sangre River sparkle and shimmer.

A large throng was gathered at its banks, talking

and laughing above the monotonous roar of the great river.

The Sangre had eaten its way through the rock of its bed, until now, after many centuries, it was deep in a gorge, a gorge which would serve as the sides to the new dam.

The town of Three Rapids was the only large level area for many miles, a plateau an hour and a half ride from the river, and had derived its name from the closeness to this spot, for in the gorge the river had eroded the earth unevenly, making its bed in three separate, dangerous steppes.

Most of the people at the ceremony were of the Gila area, both the mountain country and the basin. Rarely was there any kind of entertainment of such caliber in their lives, and they made sure that they attended, even if it meant a day's journey or more.

Yet the delegates were there, as well as dignitaries from California and New Mexico and Nevada. Governor Cardwell, unable to attend due to pressing matters in Prescott, was amply represented by a large delegation headed by Mr. Smith.

At the exact point of construction of the new dam, a large wooden parade platform had been erected and gaily decorated with red, white, and blue streamers. Several dozen folding chairs had been set up on the platform, behind a speaker's podium, to seat the delegates and dignitaries.

As Sheriff Abe McGivern remarked to Arizona Ames, beside whom he was sitting as they waited for the morning's speechmaking and officials presentations to begin, "If'n they could of found a brass band somewheres around these parts, that'd be here too."

Ames laughed appreciatively. He had grown very

202

fond of the grizzled old lawman these past few days, especially after McGivern's quick thinking had saved the Arizonan's life at Superstition Cemetery two nights previous.

It was men like McGivern, Ames reflected, who had built and would continue to build Arizona into a fine, upstanding place where a man could live with his family without fear of the likes of Neal P. Celtas, and all those like him who took no stock in human life and sneered at law and order.

"Say, Ames," McGivern said, mopping his sweating brow with a large red bandana. "There's one thing been bothering me ever since that night out in the graveyard, after we rounded up them outlaws. What with all the goings-on since, I ain't had the chance to talk to you about it till now."

"What do you want to know, sheriff?" Ames asked.

"You said you'd suspected Celtas as being behind all the raidings and killings, but I'll be durned if'n I see how."

"Three things," the Arizonan answered. "I knew that whoever was bossin' those critters had to know exactly when that money shipment was being sent from Prescott—"

"Everybody in these here parts knew that," the sheriff cut in.

"Plus the fact that I was going to Gene Cameron's that night," Ames continued. "And finally, that he would have known about the secret of Jedadiah Harrison's crypt."

"I get you now," McGivern said. "Celtas was at dinner with me, and overheard you ask directions to the nester's place, and he lived here way back when the miner was living. Why, him bein' the banker and everything, he might have handled some of the details for Harrison's tomb, Harrison swearing him to silence."

"Exactly. While there might have been other men who would have known one or another of these three things, the only person who logically knew them all was Celtas. When I heard him speak in the grotto, I knew I was right."

"Right smart thinkin', Ames," the sheriff said.

"Well, I'm just glad things worked out okay." The Arizonan looked out over the crowd, then turned back to the sheriff. "Lots of things turned out nicely, I'd say. Look yonder, at Will Franklin there."

"Where?" McGivern asked, then he said with a grin, "Oh, over by the water barrel. With his daughter and Gene Cameron. Say, you're right, Ames. I'm glad to see the three of them got together. Gene's a right fine boy, and old Will, while he's stubborner than any mule out of Missouri, ain't such a bad sort. And Priscilla—well, she's 'bout the finest looking filly in the whole of Arizona, wouldn't you say?"

Ames grinned. "If she isn't, she runs a mighty close second," he said. "I heard tell there's going to be a wedding in Three Rapids before too long."

"Yep. Will finally consented to let Gene have his daughter's hand. It should be a powerful fine ceremony and reception, Ames. You ought to try and make it."

"I will, at that."

It was along toward eleven before the festivities finally got under way, and they lasted for more than two hours, mainly because some of the chosen speakers tried to rival the hot, arid wind that blew over the damsite. But it was a fine program, and when Mr. Smith, on behalf of Governor Cardwell, presented the one hundred and fifty thousand territorial dollars to Mr. Ebenezer Toomey of the construction company which had been the successful bidder on the Sangre River Dam, the multitude of people present cheered and hooted for the better part of ten minutes.

Even Will Franklin, who had changed his tune considerably, could be seen to be shouting happily. Looking out over the crowd, Arizona Ames thought that it was odd, the way people were; superstitious and childish and frightened by a new innovation one day, they could execute a complete reversal the next. But in this case, he couldn't fault them at all, not with the erection of the Sangre River Dam meaning so much to his beloved Arizona.

A little later Ames was standing and talking to Will Franklin, congratulating Gene and Priscilla on their coming marriage and promising to attend, when Mr. Smith walked over. He smiled at the group and was introduced around by Ames, and then when the Franklins and Cameron moved on, he turned to Ames and his tone and manner dropped their joviality.

"Mr. Ames," he said earnestly, "Governor Cardwell wanted me to extend his personal thanks. He was sorry he couldn't attend this dedication, but even if he had, I'm afraid that his gratitude would have to be postponed until he meets with you again."

"Meets with me again?" the Arizonan asked.

Mr. Smith nodded. "The Territory owes you a mighty lot, and by all rights you should be able to return to Tonto Basin and bask in well deserved adulation. We can't give you that, and neither, I'm afraid, can we promise you that we won't ask you again to serve.

"The Governor wanted to have me impress upn you

205

just how high his esteem for a man of such loyalty and honesty, and yes, courage. Men like you are rare, Mr. Ames, and these are perilous times when such qualities cannot go unused.''

Mr. Smith shrugged apologetically. ''All men must serve.''

''And as best they can, Mr. Smith,'' the Arizonan said. ''Tell Governor Cardwell that I would be honored to do whatever I can for him. For him and Arizona.''

''I'm afraid you're going to have the opportunity to tell him yourself, Mr. Ames,'' Mr. Smith said. ''He's asked me to have you report to him in Prescott no later than the end of the week, at the Governor's mansion.''

''Is there some other trouble?''

''Yes, there is. I can't tell you what it is at this moment—the Governor will do that personally—but I can say this: it involves not only the security of our territory, but possibly of the entire United States of America as well.''

Ames whistled softly, reverently. ''As big as that?''

''Yes, Mr. Ames, as big as that.''

Solemnly, the Arizonan shook hands with the Governor's man.

''I'll be there, then, Mr. Smith,'' he said. ''You can count on me.''

''I knew that we could.''

As he strode toward the picnic tables piled high with food for the festivities, after having said goodbye to Mr. Smith moments later, the cowboy wondered what this new and vital trouble was. He had no inkling. All he knew was that his territory, his country, had called, and that call he must obey. This was all he needed to know.

Such was the man, Arizona Ames.

# The World's Greatest Western Writer

## ZANE GREY

Classic tales of action and adventure
set in the Old West
and penned with blistering authority
by America's Master Story Teller

THE BUFFALO HUNTER. Rugged, dangerous men and the beasts they hunted to the point of extinction.

_____2599-X                    $2.75 US/$3.75 CAN

SPIRIT OF THE BORDER. The settlers were doomed unless a few grizzled veterans of the Indian Wars, scalphunters as mean and vicious as the renegades, could stop them.

_____2564-7                    $2.75 US/$3.75 CAN

THE RUSTLERS OF PECOS COUNTY. Although outnumbered a thousand to one, the Texas Rangers were the last chance the settlers had. It had to be enough.

_____2498-5                    $2.75 US/$3.50 CAN

THE LAST RANGER. The classic frontier tale of a brutal Indian fighter and a shrewd beauty who struggled to make a heaven of the hell on earth they pioneered.

_____2447-0                    $2.95 US/$3.75 CAN

THE LAST TRAIL. White renegades stir up the hostile Indian tribes surrounding the little settlement of Fort Henry.

_____2636-8                    $2.95 US/$3.95 CAN

# The Exciting and Beloved Characters of

## ZANE GREY

### Brought to life again by his son

## ROMER ZANE GREY!

### Classic Western Action

_____2530-2  ZANE GREY'S BUCK DUANE:
KING OF THE RANGE          $2.75 US/$3.50 CAN

_____2553-1  ZANE GREY'S ARIZONA AMES: KING
OF THE OUTLAW HORDE     $2.75US/$3.50CAN

_____2488-8  ZANE GREY'S LARAMIE NELSON:
LAWLESS LAND               $2.75 US/$3.75 CAN

_____2621-7  ZANE GREY'S YAQUI: SEIGE AT
FORLORN RIVER            $2.75 US/$3.75 CAN